"I thought you'd li**said.**

Suzie stepped out of Tucker's truck and stared at the huge trees that he'd parked beneath. Cottonwoods.

"I've never seen this many of them together!" It was a beautiful sight when the cotton tuffs were floating from the branches on their slow free fall to earth. It looked like it was snowing in the middle of May!

"I've always liked this spot this time of year," Tucker said, coming to stand beside her. Smiling down at her, he plucked a bit of cotton from her hair. "It looks good on you," he said.

She wasn't thinking about the cotton any longer. "Which way will we go?" she asked, butterflies sifting inside her chest.

"Which way do you want to go?"

She stared at him, her insides completely aflutter. His deep blue eyes were steady and unwavering as they seemed to see every emotional hiding place within her.

"I don't know." Were they talking about which way to go to check fences…or something more?

Books by Debra Clopton

Love Inspired

DEBRA CLOPTON

First published in 2005, Debra Clopton is an award-winning multipublished novelist who has won a Booksellers Best Award, an Inspirational Readers' Choice Award, a Golden Quill, a *Cat-aromance* Reviewers' Choice Award, *RT Book Reviews* Book of the Year and Harlequin.com's Readers' Choice Award. She was also a 2004 finalist for the prestigious RWA Golden Heart, a triple finalist for the American Christian Fiction Writers Carol Award and most recently a finalist for the 2011 Gayle Wilson Award for Excellence.

Married for twenty-two blessed years to her high school sweetheart, Debra was widowed in 2003. Happily, in 2008, a couple of friends played matchmaker and set her up on a blind date. Instantly hitting it off, they were married in 2010. They live in the country with her husband's two high-school-age sons. Debra has two adult sons, a lovely daughter-in-law and a beautiful granddaughter—life is good! Her greatest awards are her family and spending time with them. You can reach Debra at P.O. Box 1125, Madisonville, TX 77864 or at debraclopton.com.

Her Unlikely Cowboy

Debra Clopton

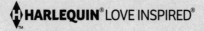

Recycling programs
for this product may
not exist in your area.

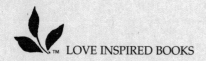 LOVE INSPIRED BOOKS

ISBN-13: 978-0-373-04286-9

HER UNLIKELY COWBOY

www.Harlequin.com

Printed in U.S.A.

Greater love hath no man than this,
that a man lay down his life for his friends.
—*John* 15:13

This book is dedicated, with much gratitude and sorrow, to the family of *and* to U.S. Marine SGT. Wade Wilson. Your sacrifice and selfless act of heroism for our freedom will not be forgotten.
1989–2012

Chapter One

More dread than hope filled Suzie Kent's heart as she drove around a wide curve toward Dew Drop, Texas. Suddenly, the flash of police lights startled her just as a mass of short, fat donkeys standing in her path yanked her out of her depressed state. Suzie gasped, "Oh!"

"Mom! Stop!" Abe yelled.

A tall man in a cowboy hat, jeans and the tan uniform of a Texas sheriff stood in the middle of the donkeys, waving his arms for her to halt. One minute he was standing, and the next—

"He went down!" Abe yelled again as the sheriff buckled and fell over.

Suzie stomped on the brakes of the monstrosity of a moving truck. The heavy vehicle groaned and rebelled, but fortunately the brakes grabbed and the bulky box on wheels lunged—once, twice, three times before stopping hard. She and Abe strained forward against their seat belts with the force.

Even intent on halting, she was shaken by what they'd witnessed. One of the cute donkeys had just taken down an officer with a well-placed kick.

Abe had his seat belt off and was out the door before Suzie even had time to tell him to be careful. At fifteen he wasn't listening to her anymore, and this was no different. Hurrying to get out of the truck, she pushed the flashers on then locked her gaze back on her son. He approached the donkeys, yelling and waving his arms wildly. She was thankful when the creatures parted down the road's yellow center stripe, scurrying like mice out of his way. This gave her a clear view of the downed officer. Sirens sounded in the distance and she hoped their shrill cry signaled help was on the way.

Abe skidded to a halt beside the black-haired man holding his hip and struggling to get up. His back was to them but it was easy to tell he was well built as he struggled to one knee, holding his injured leg straight.

"Mom, he's hurt!" Abe yelled over his shoulder, bending down and blocking her view of the officer. "I can help you stand up. If you can," he said. "That donkey blasted you."

"Thanks," the officer grunted. "That'd be much appreciated. Donkeys might be innocent-looking, but they can sure make an impact."

Though she hadn't yet glimpsed his face, Suzie quickened her pace. The officer looped his arm over Abe's shoulders just as she reached them.

"Here let me help, too." She scooted beneath his other arm, placing her hand on his stomach—his very firm stomach. The officer was in shape. Looking up she met his deep marine-blue gaze and froze.

Tucker McDermott!

"Thanks, Suzie. It's good to see you." Tucker McDermott's eyes bored into her, but concern stamped his expression, as if he knew the dismay shooting through her.

Her breath had flown from her lungs and she had no words as she looked into the face of the man she held responsible for her husband's death.

The man she was also counting on to help her save her son…. Suzie's world tilted as she realized whose clean, tangy aftershave was teasing her senses and whose unbelievably intense gaze had her insides suddenly rioting. His hair was jet-black and his skin deeply tanned, making his midnight-blue eyes startling in their intensity.

"Tucker," she managed, hoping her voice didn't wobble.

Moving to Dew Drop, Texas, to Tucker's family's Sunrise Ranch, and asking for his help had taken everything she had left emotionally—and that hadn't been much since her husband had given his life in the line of duty for fellow marine Tucker, two years earlier.

And now, as circumstances would have it, she was forced to rely on his help.

Tucker grimaced, trying to keep most of his weight off of Suzie and Abe, but his hip clearly hurt.

"Thanks for the rescue. I'm glad y'all saw the pack and stopped in time. I had just arrived and it wouldn't have been good if you'd wrecked because of these hairy pests."

Suzie realized the donkey must have kicked him in his bad hip.

Shot.

The word ricocheted through her. He'd

been shot in the hip and gone down in a firefight—a firefight after being ambushed.

The firefight in which her husband, Gordon, had stepped in front of him and drawn fire.

Acid rolled in the pit of her stomach thinking about it.

"Thank y'all for helping me up," he said, his gaze snagging on hers again and holding. "I've got it from here, though." He pulled one arm from around her and the other from around Abe.

"Are you sure?" she asked, even though she wanted to step away from him in the worst way. Wanted to break the disturbing connection radiating between them. "Do we need to help you to your vehicle?

"Yeah," Abe added, looking just as uncertain as she did.

Tucker limped a few painful steps away from them. "I'm okay," he said, gruffly. "It'll just take a few minutes for the throbbing to go away." He glanced ruefully at the donkeys. "What a mess."

"There's a bunch of them," Abe said excitedly, accepting Tucker at his word and moving back to focus on the herd of innocent-looking donkeys.

Suzie's heart caught. Abe's reaction—from the first moment they'd spotted the donkeys—was the first time in weeks, even months, that she'd heard any kind of positive excitement in his voice. Now he was actually grinning at the short, squat animals.

"They act like they own the road," he added, looking as if he wanted to pet one of them.

Tucker frowned. "And that's the problem. They could easily have caused a serious wreck."

"They sure took you out." Abe chuckled.

Suzie suddenly felt as though she was in a time warp, glimpsing the son she'd had before his father died. A lump lodged in her throat and her eyes welled with tears. She fought both down.

Tucker's lip hitched upward in a quick lopsided grin. "It's my own fault. A donkey's God-given instinct is to kick and they have a range of motion that would surprise a prize fighter. That's why they're used to protect herds from predators."

"Seriously?" Abe gaped at Tucker then at the docile, unassuming animals.

"Seriously," Tucker said. "They may not look like much, but those are some kickboxing masters right there."

"Cool," Abe said, swinging around as, siren blaring, a Dew Drop Sheriff's Department car rolled to a halt beside Tucker's SUV. "Looks like backup has arrived."

A young officer emerged from his patrol car, and strode their way. "Hey, Tucker, got here as soon as I could." A cocky grin widened across his suntanned skin. "Couldn't handle the misfit delinquents yourself?"

Delinquent. The word hit Suzie in the

heart and wiped the smile off Abe's face instantly. He'd become too acquainted with the term of late, and the mention was all it took for shadows of mistrust to cloud his blue eyes. She almost cried out as she saw the veil of anger fall, the veil that he'd disappeared behind months ago. Her gaze shot to Tucker and she realized that he'd witnessed Abe's reaction.

"Yeah, the donkeys are troublemakers, all right," he clarified smoothly. "Help me get them off the road, Cody," he instructed the deputy, then focused on Abe. "By the way, I'm Tucker McDermott. I was a friend of your dad's and I owe him my life. He was an amazing man." Tucker cleared his throat. "I'm glad you've come to Dew Drop. And the boys of Sunrise Ranch are looking forward to meeting you."

Abe's expression flashed bright with anger as he stared at Tucker, then, glaring daggers at the deputy, he stalked back toward their moving truck. "This is ridiculous, Mom. Why'd we have to come here?"

Her mild-looking, blue-eyed, blond-haired son was a time bomb. Feeling sick, she glanced back at Tucker. He hadn't moved and was still favoring his hip. She wasn't sure he could move. "Tell me this is going to work out."

The weight of the world—her world—settled heavily on her and she felt suddenly weary and far, far older than her thirty-two years.

Tucker's fierce gaze engulfed her. "You have my word, Suzie. This is going to work out. I promise."

Tears sprang to her eyes, and all she could do was nod. She was so tired of handling everything on her own. So very tired. Tucker was offering her a strong support system and strong words that she needed to believe in.

"Hey, Abe," he called. "Could you help

us herd these donkeys off the road before someone gets hurt?"

Abe spun back, his stance still belligerent but his expression interested. "Sure."

Tearing her gaze from her son, she looked back at Tucker, amazed.

"I hate to ask," Tucker said, as if nothing out of the ordinary had just happened—but surely he knew it had. "Could you help, too? I'm not moving as fast as I need to and we need them off this road. The trailer will be here soon but..."

"Um, yes, just tell me what to do."

"Move slow and wave your arms if one starts to come at you. Contrary to what you witnessed, they aren't aggressive. They're pretty tame. Until you sneak up on them like I did. Or try to ride them. I hear they don't like that at all."

"Okay." She glanced at Abe, who was already urging a group of three to move toward the edge of the road. "Abe, be careful," she called.

"Mom, I've got this," he huffed, impatient with her mothering.

"I'll get this end," the other officer called from where he'd moved to the far side of the group.

That left the middle of the herd for her and Tucker. Feeling that she wasn't doing it right, she waved her arms somewhat weakly, moving toward the donkey closest to her.

Not intimidated in the least, fuzzy whiskers lifted her way and deep brown eyes studied her. Clearly distracted from nuzzling the yellow line, the animal blinked dark eyelashes, pawed the pavement twice—then *charged.*

Suzie gasped, her arms dropped like lead as she spun and ran—straight into Tucker McDermott's arms.

"Hold on," Tucker said, pulling her protectively against his body and shifting so the crazy donkey aimed at him instead of her.

"Yah!" he yelled at the miserable beast and waved his arm in a not-so-weak manner.

The donkey skidded to a halt instantly.

Tucker held her tightly with one arm and shooed the silly animal away. It turned and trotted off, as if it hadn't just tried to mow her down.

"They just get excited sometimes. No harm meant," Tucker assured her. His soft chuckle washed over her. "It's okay."

Suzie was mortified that she'd run to him. That she was now in his arms. And her crazy heart was pounding, even as his low rumbling chuckle resonated through her. What was wrong with her? She was reacting to Tucker's touch as if…as if she were attracted to him. Even the thought made her ill, made her feel like a traitor.

True, she hadn't been held like this in almost three years because when Gordon died it'd been months since she'd seen him. But still, *Tucker McDermott*.

This was disturbing and wrong on so

many levels that she couldn't stand it. Yet, even as she worried, Tucker's aftershave, manly and teasing, filled her senses as he soothingly rubbed her back.

This was the man she held responsible for her husband's death.

"You're trembling."

"Yes," she forced, pulling away. "I'm not used to charging animals. And I'm embarrassed. I don't make a habit of running into strange men's arms."

He looked confused. "You don't have anything to be embarrassed about. You didn't know. If an animal does that again, yell loud and make an aggressive move of your own. It will run for the hills. Usually."

Like she hadn't tried that. "Fine," she snapped. "Thanks, um, for the lesson. I believe I'll wait in the truck." She stumbled over her words, turned and strode toward the van, daring even one of the measly animals to come her way! It was all she could do not to run as humiliation and indignation collided.

Yanking the door of the moving truck open, she climbed inside, glancing out at Abe as she tried to compose herself. He appeared sullen but, surprisingly, continued helping move the varmints off the road. Her gaze shifted back to Tucker. His expression was grim as he stared after her, probably wondering why she was acting so strange.

After a moment he turned away, and she watched him take a step, stiff at first, then better after a couple of steps. Still, though his expression didn't show it, she sensed he was in real pain.

Good.

The mean-spirited thought jumped into her mind instantaneously. Shame engulfed her. She'd been outspoken in the past, when needed, but never mean-spirited.

Death changed a person. Hardened up the heart like a cement block—she hated it.

She hated everything about this process of loss and its life-altering aftermath.

The truth was, she had no choice but to be here and hope with all her heart that Tucker McDermott and the Sunrise Ranch could help her son. Abe was the only reason she was here.

Her fifteen-year-old was hurting so bad on the inside that the only way he could cope was to lash out in ways that scared her for him. Her son, who needed more than she'd been able to give him.

Over the phone when she'd spoken with Tucker, before coming here, he'd given her his word that all would be well. She was praying that Tucker's word meant as much as Gordon believed it meant…

Gordon had been a few years younger than Tucker when he'd come to live at Tucker's family's ranch. A working cattle ranch that was also a foster home for boys who'd been abandoned and were alone in the world. Gordon had looked up to Tucker and he'd told her he'd become a marine because Tucker was a marine.

Gordon would have walked through fire for Tucker and had told her if anything ever happened to him she should turn to him for help.

As it turned out, her husband had given his life for Tucker…

And left her to raise their son alone.

Tucker McDermott was the last person she wanted to turn to for help, but her son was in trouble and Suzie would do whatever it took to save him.

An hour after he'd been kicked, Tucker watched the trailer loaded with donkeys drive away. His hip throbbed like the pounding of a heavy-metal band…and since he had a metal plate in his thigh, it stood to reason. It was feeling better, he thought as he eased into the seat and closed the door. Totally conscious that he was being watched from the rented moving truck twenty yards away, he turned off his lights, backed up, then headed toward the ranch with Suzie following.

He'd been shaken to look down at the flaxen-haired woman helping him and discover Suzie Kent's remarkable blue-green eyes.

So much had crashed through his mind at that moment. Guilt for being alive when her husband was dead. Sorrow for what the war had cost her and her son—and Gordon. But there was the other emotion that swept through him strong and swift and deep… attraction.

Gordon had shown him her picture over and over when they were stationed in the Middle East. No one in the unit had missed seeing Suzie's photo. He'd been so proud and so in love with her. And Tucker could completely understand why—not just because of how beautiful she was, but because of the person his comments set her up to be. She'd sounded like a kind and caring woman, and her actions proved it. She didn't just send letters to her husband, but also care packages filled with his favorite things. And she always sent along plenty for the other marines in his unit—a thoughtful gesture appreciated by all.

Suzie Kent was the real deal and Gordon had been a lucky man.

Tucker hadn't been so lucky in love, before his stint in the marines or since. He'd been too in love with his career—this had been pointed out to him several times and it had been true. Driven to make a difference in the world was what he'd called it.

He wasn't marriage material back then, still wasn't. But he knew finding what Gordon and Suzie had found together wasn't easy.

He'd been happy for Gordon, though, and drawn to look at Suzie's pictures as often as Gordon wanted to show them. Everything was raw and harsh and brutal where they'd been, and looking into Suzie Kent's sparkling eyes had made him feel that there was hope in this world.

That he was fighting for goodness to prevail.

Moments ago, Tucker had looked down and Suzie hadn't been a photo any longer. She'd been real, and staring into her eyes, brutal reality had struck him like a bolt of lightning. Suzie Kent had once been full of life, fun and vivacious. Now she was sad and struggling to hide it.

Worry was etched into her expression and imprinted in the depths of her eyes. She seemed skittish, too, and uncertain.

And it was because of him.

If he'd died and Gordon had lived, she wouldn't be having the trouble she was having with her son or her life.

And, as much as he wanted to help Abe, Tucker wanted just as much to bring back the girl in those photos.

He knew deep in his soul that Gordon would have wanted that.

And as he began the drive toward the ranch with Suzie following, Tucker vowed once more that he would not let his fallen friend down.

Chapter Two

Turmoil rolled in Suzie's stomach like bad chicken salad as she followed Tucker down the country road. Pastures spread out on either side of the road, and yellow flowers were everywhere, carpeting the hillside in sunny yellow—goatweed, she knew, but pretty nonetheless.

When a majestic, wooden entrance came into view she knew this was Sunrise Ranch before she saw the name and before Tucker slowed and turned into the drive. Gordon had described everything perfectly.

In the distance, she could see the tops of the ranch buildings. She didn't look at Abe, but she felt him straighten in his seat and bend forward slightly, as if to get a better view. Her heart squeezed tight with hope.

They topped the hill, and the ranch spread out before them.

"This is where your dad came to live about the age you are now," she said, even though he already knew this. "He loved it here. I can see why."

Abe had stopped talking much about Gordon over the past year. It was as if he were angry with him for not being around. She understood. She had her own anger issues to deal with.

"Your dad had described it just like this," she said, loving the look of the place as she pulled to a halt beside Tucker at the rear of the large ranch house—a welcoming two-story house with an expansive back porch, inviting one to sit a spell overlooking the ranch compound. Out to the side of the house, an office and then a chow hall sat connected by porches and plank sidewalks.

Small wooden signs swinging from the covered porches confirmed this, but she knew it from Gordon's descriptions.

Directly across the white rock parking lot was an older, but extremely well-maintained red stable that he'd said was at least a hundred years old. Gordon had loved the stable—she could still hear the awe in his tone when he talked of the baby horses being born there.

Beside the stable was a massive silver barn with an arena and corral attached. And out in the distance sat another building with playground equipment behind it—this was the schoolhouse.

There were boys everywhere, it seemed. Some were in the arena with a few cattle, others were on horses, riding toward them across the pasture. No sooner had Suzie parked than it seemed their truck was surrounded.

Suzie could easily tell that the bright-eyed boys were all ages, the youngest seemed to be eight or nine but there were all heights and ages.

Surely one of these boys would be a good friend to Abe.

She was about to open her door, but a dark-headed kid who looked amazingly like a young Elvis pulled it open for her.

"Hi, ma'am. Welcome to Sunrise Ranch. I'm Tony."

She could not help but smile. Not only from the fact that he did, indeed, sound like Elvis, but also because just the simple act of courtesy gave her another swift surge of hope. His eyes twinkled with goodwill and happiness—as her Abe's once had. *Please, God, let this be the answer.*

She heard Abe's door squeak open and glanced over her shoulder to see him getting out. Tucker was exiting his truck at the same time and said something to him as Abe closed his door. She turned back and smiled at Tony and the other boys, all talking at the same time.

"You done brung us another boy," said a small, plump boy, who looked to be the youngest. He looked from her to Abe on the other side of the truck.

"You want us to show you how to rope?" one called to Abe.

"Are you going to live here?"

"Can you ride a horse?"

Questions bombarded them from all directions.

She laughed, not knowing who to answer first.

"Whoa, boys," Tucker said, rounding the end of the truck with Abe. "Take it slow. This here is Abe. Yes, he's going to be going to school with y'all. And yes, he'll also need some help learning to ride and rope and work cows."

Suzie watched as everyone started introducing themselves. It was going to take her forever to learn all of their names. She *would* remember Tony. He seemed to be close to Abe's age.

Over the tops of their heads, her gaze met Tucker's and her pulse kicked into a gallop. His deep blue eyes seemed to reach for her and she felt suddenly breathless. What was wrong with her? These were emotions of attraction.

And they had no place between her and Tucker McDermott.

No place at all.

Abruptly the office door opened, and a tall, straight-backed woman with a gray pony-tail and a wide grin came striding outside— Ruby Ann McDermott. She was followed by Randolph McDermott. Both had come to Gordon's funeral and stood beside her as if they were his family. They'd loved Gordon and he'd loved them, having considered them the family he'd never had since his parents abandoned him early in life. At the service, they'd given their condolences and offered to help her in any way they could. She'd refused their help at the time.

Randolph, a handsome man in his mid-fifties had threads of white at the temples of his charcoal hair. He'd marked his sons with the same dark hair and George Strait good looks.

Crossing to her now, she was struck again by his kind eyes as he took her hand in his.

"We are so glad you've come," he said. "We loved Gordon and are honored to get the opportunity to know you and Abe through Sunrise Ranch. This was Gordon's home and he loved it here."

"Thank you. He did love it."

Ruby Ann, or Nana as Gordon said he and all the boys affectionately called her, wrapped her arms around Suzie, just as she'd done at the funeral two years earlier. "Welcome to Sunrise Ranch, precious girl," she said. "I'm so glad you've come. We all are."

Randolph's eyes held hers. "We are forever in Gordon's debt for the sacrifice he made, and the sacrifice you and Abe made. His home is your home."

She fought back tears, her emotions were on edge today. She'd heard so many similar declarations over the past two years. But none of them changed what had happened.

And yet people were sincere, and that meant so much to her.

"Thank you. And I'm very grateful for what you're doing for us. For Abe," she said softly, not wanting him to hear, though he was now encircled by the other boys and she doubted he could hear anything she might say. Her heart swelled with gratefulness, despite the turmoil raging inside of her at having to turn to Tucker. Without the hope they were giving her with this opportunity for Abe she didn't know what she would have done.

Nana smiled warmly. "You think nothing of it. That boy needs this place. I can feel it in my soul. There's healing here at Sunrise Ranch. You needn't worry. Time and God's goodness will heal his broken heart."

Glancing back at Abe she caught Tucker's

gaze again. A shiver raced down her spine when she thought she glimpsed pain in his eyes. She looked away and was glad when Randolph and Nana moved in to meet Abe.

She pushed aside the thought that Tucker might be hurting, too—and not just in his wounded hip. For two years she'd blamed him, never once thinking about what he'd been through, and now, upon meeting him, she had started thinking about his feelings.

It made her nervous and she wasn't sure why. She hadn't had long to think about it when one of the littler boys tugged on her arm.

"We're gonna show you and your boy how to rodeo," he said. "Oh, and I'm Sammy." A wide, enthusiastic smile spread big and bright across his thin face, and he puffed his chest way out. "I'm gettin' good and I've only been here a little over a year. Just think how good I'm going to be next month."

She laughed. He was so adorable and it was obvious he was thriving here.

To her surprise, the boys had planned a mini rodeo for them and, within minutes, in the midst of a flurry of action, she and Abe found themselves over by the arena watching the boys riding their horses and roping and chasing calves. Abe looked sullen, but at least he wasn't storming off to be alone.

"So, we're all excited you bought Joyce and Lester's flower shop," Nana said, coming to stand beside her at the arena fence.

"I am, too." Finding the flower shop for sale had been a bonus incentive for coming to Dew Drop. It wasn't as if she could just pick up and move to the town without a job to support them. That had been a worry. But she'd worked at a florist's for years, and when she'd started looking at possible jobs she'd come across the for-sale ad for the Dew Drop Petal. The price had been unbelievably reasonable, and she'd known exactly what to use part of her life insurance settlement on.

The flower shop had been a great blessing. And after feeling as though God had turned his back on them since Gordon's death, it had been very welcoming to her bruised faith.

"Dew Drop's not that big, but you should do well. And if there is anything I can do, I'd be happy to help. And our Tucker there, he'll assist you any way he can. That man has a huge cloud of guilt hanging over his head where Gordon is concerned. He loved Gordon as a brother. He'll want to help you in any way he can."

Suzie didn't want to think about his guilty feelings. "I came here for him to help with Abe. That's all I'll need from him."

Nana studied her with deep blue eyes that unsettled her. After a moment, she patted Suzie's arm. "God's got a plan, Suzie. I think maybe you don't believe that. But He does. He always does."

Suzie yanked her gaze away and, without meaning to, found herself looking at the broad-shouldered form of Tucker leaning on the fence beside Abe, pointing at the boys, explaining to her son what was going on in the arena.

She was clinging to the hope of a plan, but it didn't have anything to do with spending unnecessary time with Tucker McDermott.

As a matter of fact, the less time she spent around him, the better.

"Hey, you want me to show you how to rope?"

Tucker took a swig of his iced tea. The cold, sweet liquid did nothing to cool the burning tension in the pit of his stomach as Abe gave Caleb an angry glare. Caleb was trying to pull Abe out of his shell, but the boy wasn't interested. Fortunately, the boys of Sunrise Ranch were used to this kind of behavior and had probably been on the giving end when they'd first arrived at the ranch, alone, lost and feeling as if their world had come to an end.

The emotions that warred behind Abe's chilly blue gaze were not uncommon.

Tucker's dad always halted chores and school and held some small welcome event for each boy upon his arrival, to showcase the fun that was in store for him. This helped ease their transition and break them into life on the ranch by snagging their interest.

During the mini rodeo for Abe and Suzie, Tucker spent time explaining what each event was to Abe. Though the kid hadn't joined in on the conversation, the fact that he'd listened was a plus, and Tucker believed he was interested.

When the rodeo was over, Nana called everyone to the chow hall, where they'd decided to have their first meal with Suzie and Abe. Sometimes Nana would have the guests and all the boys over at the house, but it was a rowdy event and they'd decided it would be better to eat in the chow hall. It would be good for Suzie to see where Abe would be having his meals during school hours. Abe would eat supper at the ranch house with Suzie and Nana, since the boys ate their evening meal with their house parents at the two foster homes on the ranch.

Tucker had given Suzie some space not long after the mini rodeo started, staying out of her way for a couple of hours. She was clearly not comfortable around him, and so he'd let his dad and his grandmother and his other family members try to put her at ease. His brother Morgan was there with his wife, Jolie, who was the teacher of the school. And his youngest brother, Rowdy, was there also, though his fiancée, Lucy, was at an art show in New York and couldn't make it. Everyone had tried hard to make Suzie and Abe feel welcome and she'd seemed to respond well with them. Even seemed to relax and he'd thought some of the tension had eased from her eyes.

But dinner was over now. Pans of home-made lasagna and Nana's handmade rolls had been devoured and only the crumbs remained. The huge bowls of her cream-cheese banana pudding slathered in whipped cream were practically licked clean. And the boys were walking around smacking their lips in satisfaction.

His nana knew how to make boys happy. She gave them plenty of love and nurturing, and filled them with the best food in Texas, and plenty of it.

As the sun started to dip under the horizon, he knew it was time to talk; he'd put it off as long as possible.

Suzie and Nana were on the porch, and as he walked over he forced the nerves rattling around in his gut like barbed wire to go away. He'd faced more than his share of danger, and yet facing Suzie made him feel like a coward.

"I hate to interrupt, but, Suzie, could we take a walk? I think it would be a good idea for us to discuss a few things."

She minded. It was written clearly in her eyes.

"No, not at all. If you'll excuse me, Nana, Tucker is right. We need to talk."

Nana squeezed Suzie's arm. "You go along, dear. When you get back I'll show you upstairs to your room and you can get you and Abe settled into the ranch house."

"Thanks. Thanks for everything."

Nana waved off the gratitude. "You are family, just like Gordon was. My house is your house. Helping is what families do. Now go, it will do the two of you good to talk."

There were kids all around the yard and the barn, and despite Abe's reluctance to join in, Tony and Caleb, along with Jake, one of the newest teens, had gotten him to go to the stable to see the horses. Horses were always good for the boys.

"We can walk out to the school, if you'd like. I'm sure you'd like to see where Abe will be tomorrow."

Placing her hand on her stomach, as if to calm her nerves, she nodded and fell into step with him.

In her running shoes, she came to just below his chin. So when she looked at him she was looking up slightly and it made her seem even more vulnerable than he knew she was.

"How's Abe doing since we talked?" They'd had a couple of conversations on the phone prior to her move. She'd explained that she needed help, that Abe was hanging with a crowd of older boys who were constantly in trouble and that she was afraid for him. He'd heard the fear and distress in her voice over the long-distance line.

Two of the boys Abe had been hanging out with had just been sent to juvenile jail. Abe had been sneaking out at night, several times that she knew of, and he refused to tell her what he'd been doing. She'd called Tucker out of desperation and he knew it— because she blamed him for Gordon being dead. She'd made that clear when he'd gone to see her after being released from the hospital. She'd refused his help and refused to have anything to do with him.

Until now.

Her eyes flashed and he could have punched himself.

"You saw him," she said tightly. "He's like a bomb waiting to explode. He's been that way since he lost his father. It's just getting worse." The accusation vibrated in her words and the vein in her throat beat so hard it was obvious that her blood pressure had skyrocketed. He hated that he'd done this. His own blood was pounding in his ears. He hadn't been trained for this.

Silence stretched between them, the only sound the soft crunch of gravel as they followed the path across the pasture toward the school.

He started over. "What I meant to say was—how long after losing his father was it before he started hanging around this group of kids?"

Her shoulders slumped as she pushed her silky hair behind her ear. "It was about a year ago. We'd had a tough first year. Lots of tears and angry outbursts and sullenness. We saw a counselor, but Abe wouldn't open up and eventually he refused to return. I should have found him another counselor— one he would talk to. I should have continued until I found the right one. But he refused and said if I took him to another one, he would run away. And I believed him."

There was anguish in her voice and it tore at Tucker. He said a silent prayer that God would lead him in helping Suzie. His faith had been the strength that had sustained him through all of this. His faith that God would not let this family down.

"I understand. And after that?"

She took a deep breath. "After that, things went downhill. He started skipping school and sneaking out at night, even though he was barely thirteen. He was in detention much of the time. The school tried. They felt for him. He met one of these boys in detention. The other was a dropout."

"You can't blame yourself."

She looked up at him. "I don't."

Her eyes were hard where he'd seen softness and love in the photos of her smiling at her husband. Tucker's gut clenched and he felt like throwing up.

"At least I try not to. I blame the war. I blame you. Even though I know it's unreasonable. I do. But still, I feel guilty because I couldn't hold it together without Gordon. He was made of stauncher stuff. He believed in me. And in the end, I've let him down." Tears were in her eyes. "He believed in you, too. And so I've come. Maybe his trust in you is worth more than his trust in me."

Her throat worked as she tried not to cry.

It was clear in her expression that she was fighting breaking down.

"No, it isn't," he offered bluntly, feeling awkward. How was he supposed to answer something like that? "I'm sure you're probably exhausted from the move, too," he said, when she looked away as if embarrassed that she was crying. It took everything Tucker had not to wipe away the tears trailing down her cheeks. He vowed he would fix this as best it could be fixed without Gordon rising from the dead.

She wiped away the tears herself and took a shuddering breath. He watched her stiffen her shoulders.

He cleared his own throat. "Your husband loved you more than life itself. It was evident to all who came within ten feet of him. Your picture was shown around more than a pinup, and he talked about how strong and good you were. He would never believe you let him down. You should know that."

She looked away. "If we don't find a way

to save Abe from this destructive path he's on, nothing else matters. Sunrise Ranch and you are my last hope."

"We'll all get through. This is a place of healing. My mother had a dream to see scared and scarred boys find a place to belong and mend. She knew…" He paused and looked across the pastures at the setting sun and the beauty surrounding them. When he looked back at Suzie she had followed his gaze and was staring toward the sunset, too.

"You've seen the boys who are here. They are happy, regular boys now. Yes, they have deep hurts and issues that they deal with, but we are their support group. Their family. Just as Gordon was part of our family. You saw some of that tonight with Nana. Even if no one else makes any headway with Abe, Nana and her food and love will smooth a path for others to reach him. It happens all the time."

They started walking again. "She is wonderful." There was wistful hope in her voice.

That breathless sound eased a knot slightly that had formed beneath his rib cage. They'd reached the school and stopped beside the porch. "She is," he agreed. "So rest assured. And I promise it will work out. It may not be easy but Abe will be all right." He'd never made promises he meant more than the ones he was making to Suzie.

Tucker prayed God's plan and his plan were the same.

"Let me show you the school," he said, opening the door. "It's a simple three-room structure with restrooms." They walked into the large, open room full of desks and bookshelves and exploding with color. "As you know, Jolie is the teacher. And she loves bright colors."

She paused in the doorway, and her breath caught. "I love it! It radiates with happiness. Just like she does."

Glad for something positive to latch on to, he smiled looking at some of the bulletin boards. "That's true, Jolie is a very happy person and it shows. Jolie loves color and light. She had Rowdy's fiancée, Lucy, paint the mural of the outdoor scene around the chalkboard."

"I love that. It brings the outside in."

He was feeling hopeful now, hearing the excitement in Suzie's voice. "She loves the outdoors, and holds class outside a lot. At her request we added more picnic tables out back under the trees. She's great."

"She and Morgan were really nice at dinner. I heard the boys saying she was a champion kayaker."

"Yes. World-class. But her heart is here now. The boys are enthralled with her."

"I can see why. It's rather intimidating to think about."

"Tell me about it. I certainly don't know how kayakers do what they do, and I don't want to. But the boys like the idea that their teacher has an adventurous spirit. It helps her to be able to talk to them. Plus, she was raised here. Her parents were house parents, and she went to school here with me, Morgan and Rowdy, when the school first started. She has witnessed the power of Sunrise Ranch. She'll be good for Abe."

Suzie nodded. "I like that. This is certainly going to be different than the school he was attending."

"We found having a smaller group setting was a better option for the boys here at the ranch. It will be good for Abe." He prayed it was so.

He showed her the rest of the school, then took her out back to the picnic tables and swings that sat beneath the oak trees. A breeze rustled through the leaves, and the sunset had turned into a pink glow, making a beautiful horizon.

Suzie turned to him. "Thank you for agreeing to do this."

He could tell that was costing her. What must she feel about him behind those beautiful, sad eyes?

Tucker yanked his thoughts back. He had

a good head on his shoulders. He knew how to handle tough situations and make clear decisions under stressful ones. The emotions assaulting him as he stared into Suzie's eyes were dangerous. Having a crush on the wife of the man whose death you felt responsible for just was not acceptable.

And if she even got a hint of what he was feeling, she would surely leave this ranch and never come back.

And he wouldn't blame her at all.

Chapter Three

"Abe, can I come in?" Suzie asked, tapping softly on the door of his room. There was a muffled "Whatever" from the other side of the door, so she opened it. Abe was stretched out on the bed staring at the ceiling. The fluffy green bedspread made him seem small, even though she knew he was growing like a weed.

She walked across the room and sat down on the edge of the bed. He kept his gaze firmly locked on the ceiling, and didn't even glance at her. Her fingers itched to push the lock of hair out of his eyes.

"I just wanted to tell you good-night." She

touched his arm gently, but he pulled away. The boy she'd glimpsed earlier on the road with the donkeys seemed like a dream gone away. As if she'd imagined him for a moment. "The boys seem nice. Tony and Caleb must be about your age, too."

His jaw tightened. "They're okay," he said at last. "Now can I go to sleep?"

"Abe, I won't have you being disrespectful," she said, shaken by his coldness. His eyes suddenly glistened with unshed tears. Her heart broke one more time.... How could a heart break over and over again? How...? *Dear God, help me. Help my son.*

After a moment she stood, knowing that hugging him was asking too much.

"Abe, what happened to us—losing your father—that wasn't fair. But life isn't fair always. Your dad would want you to be happy. This ranch, these people. They made him happy. I just want you to give it all a chance."

His gaze met hers finally, but only for a

desolate moment, then he rolled over and turned his back to her.

"I love you, son." It felt like she was saying the words to a brick wall. Her heart ached.

Abe's going to be all right. I promise. Tucker's words echoed through her thoughts and gave her strength.

Still, it took everything in her to stand up, walk out and close the door.

Tomorrow a new day would begin.

And Suzie was going to trust that it would be their new start. She was going to think positive and give it everything she had. For Abe.

The next morning, Suzie's sense of hope continued to prevail as she drove into town. Abe had eaten a huge breakfast with the other boys—Nana relayed the info, because Suzie had forced herself not to hover. Not to go peek through the windows, either— though it was exactly what she wanted to do.

Sometimes a mother's job was hard—stepping back was one of the harder things.

But when she'd walked across the hall to his room she'd been surprised to find him already up and dressed and she'd taken that as a great sign. He'd startled her more by revealing that he'd decided to help feed the horses.

Evidently he'd been invited to do so, and after a night of thinking about it, he'd decided to help. It was a positive start and Suzie, not knowing what to expect when she'd awakened that morning, was thrilled.

Now, heading into town, she found herself relaxing in the seat of her small car, which Tucker had unhitched from the moving truck the previous night. She had the truck for another day, so she was going to have to find a place to rent, though the McDermotts had assured her that she and Abe were welcome to stay as long as needed. And she was wondering if prolonging their stay for a little while might be a good thing, if spending mornings, days and nights there would put him more in the action for a little while.

There was an apartment on the second story of the building that housed the florist's shop, but she'd been told it was in some disrepair. She wasn't sure she wanted to live above the store, anyway—how good would that be for Abe? But it was an option.

For now, she'd use it to store her things until she decided what she wanted to do.

The town was darling. The four-story, redbrick Dew Drop Inn reigned supreme across from a quaint town park that was surrounded by four rows of small businesses. On the far corner across the street from the Dew Drop Inn was the Spotted Cow Café with a sunny yellow door and red geraniums. Like a welcome sign, it begged a person to come visit.

On the bench outside the newspaper office just down the street sat two older gentlemen who waved as she passed. They were whittling and added to the feeling that Mayberry had come to life. Suzie instantly imagined Sheriff Andy Taylor walking the streets— but then, Tucker McDermott's image replaced the fictional sheriff's image and Dew Drop seemed suddenly a little more exciting than Mayberry. *Stop with that, already!*

Pulling into the empty parking spot three doors down from the weathered church pew where the gentlemen were sitting, a wave of nerves suddenly attacked her like stinging bees.

The ugly chipped door of her new business was directly in front of her, kind of a toss-up between mud-brown and murky gray.

"First order of business," she muttered. "Paint that door."

To say it was bad was the understatement of the year. And hopefully not a foreshadowing of things to come once she opened it and stepped inside.

The two older men came hurrying down the sidewalk, their boots scuffing as they came.

"We've been expecting you this morning," the taller one said, grinning wide. He looked as though he smiled often because of the crinkles around his pale green eyes. "We made sure and got here early, just so we could welcome you. Right, Drewbaker?"

"Right, Chili," the other man agreed. "We usually show up in the afternoon after we get our cows fed, but we snuck away this morning." He winked, making her chuckle at the pure teasing in his manner.

"Thank you so much for coming. I'm Suzie Kent."

"Oh, we know who you are. But I'm Chili Crump and that's Drewbaker Mackintosh."

Mr. Mackintosh nodded. "We heard all about you buying the place from Joyce and Lester. Those two were so excited to hook a buyer, they told the world it had sold before the papers were signed."

"Ain't that the truth," Mr. Crump said, scratching his jaw. "Why, they packed up their motor home and left town almost before we could wave goodbye. You'd think they couldn't wait to get rid of us."

Mr. Mackintosh's entire face fell with his frown. "Yeah, kind of felt like we weren't wanted anymore," he said, then winked again. "They really wanted to get out of town before you changed your mind."

"That bad?" she asked, enjoying herself, despite the ominous teasing.

Both men grinned and followed her to the door, watching as she stuck in the key. Opening the door felt as if she was opening the best gift at Christmas, even as the musty scent of age wafted out in greeting.

"Well, gentlemen, let's see what I've got, shall we?" She couldn't help but feel happy walking in. Comical expressions of doom and gloom lit her new friends' faces—half teasing, she knew, and yet the place had certainly seen better times.

Entering, she had to step lively to get out of their way as they crowded in behind her.

Someone flicked the lights on—not really a good thing, since it illuminated the lost and forlorn look of the empty flower shop. Glass cases that had to be some of the first ever made lined one wall. A single forgotten vase of flowers sat wilted behind the glass. The floors were old planks, rough and worn so that they had a shine to them like pebbles under a constant stream of water. Their footsteps rang out in the cavernous room.

The back room wasn't any better. The tables all looked as though they were made from leftover wood, with plywood tops that had no charm at all. Turning back to the front room she studied the small front counter, more of a podium, with barely enough room for a purchase tablet much less a computer—even a small laptop. That would have to be remedied. Bad, to say the least, and yet…light streamed in from the large, old plate-glass window and made a sunny spot in the center of the room. It was to that sunny spot that Suzie walked and stood as she readjusted her eyes.

"It ain't much to look at."

"Mr. Mackintosh, you're right, it has its bad points."

"Call me Drewbaker. Ever'body does."

"And the same here. Call me Chili, little lady."

She smiled. "Drewbaker and Chili, then. It does have its bad points. But, for the money I paid, I got a steal of a deal. That's a huge plus. And look up. Isn't that tin ceiling amazing? What charm."

Both of them cranked their necks back and frowned.

"You've got better eyes than me," Drewbaker said. "Ain't no charm in here."

Chili agreed with his silence and the skeptical expression on his craggy face.

"Now, it's not that bad," Tucker said from the doorway. "Good morning, Suzie. Fellas."

Suzie's pulse bucked into rodeo mode upon seeing him—it was very disturbing.

"Good morning," she said. Then, not waiting for any more encouraging declarations, she walked over to the glass cases and tried the sliding doors. "These work great. That's a plus. They would be the most expensive pieces for me to purchase, so as long as they keep the flowers cool, everything else is workable. You'll be amazed what a little paint will do."

"That's right," Tucker said, coming over to test the doors himself. "You have a great attitude."

"Well, I have two choices. See only the bad or start thinking positive. I want to think positive. Paint will work wonders. And scrubbing and rearranging.

"And flowers," she added. "Flowers everywhere will change the whole atmosphere."

And scent. What was that odor?

Candles. Candles and flowers would change the scent.

Yes, she had a plan.

She dropped her fists to her hips and did a full turn, taking in the room, trying not to think about Tucker watching her.

She came to a halt at the comical expressions of dismay on Chili's and Drewbaker's faces.

"This place is a dump. To tell you the truth, we haven't been in here in years." Drewbaker scratched his head. "My wife always said I'd pick a neighbor's rose and give it to her before I'd pay for one, and I reckon she was right."

Suzie chuckled. "Sadly, you aren't alone."

"I bought a few in my day," Chili said, with a sheepish grin. "But it's been a while. I might have to buy some once you get this joint up and going. Matter of fact, you put me down as your first customer. You just let me know when you start making deliveries."

Tucker shot him a glance.

"You're serious?" Drewbaker asked.

"I am. A man's got to make a move some-time."

Drewbaker's laugh nearly busted out the windows. "Well, I'll be getting me some entertainment from this. What do you think, Tucker?"

"Might be interesting," Tucker agreed, his eyes dancing with laughter.

Suzie couldn't help but be curious, but she'd learned not to ask personal questions about flowers unless it was absolutely necessary. Privacy was part of her business. So she'd wait. "I'll certainly let you know the date," she said.

"Okay, Romeo," Drewbaker grunted. "You and me both have hungry cows waitin' on us. We bes' get a move on."

The two said their goodbyes and were gone, leaving Suzie and Tucker alone. The room seemed suddenly much smaller than it had before.

"How long have you been a florist?" he asked. "You seem to really enjoy it."

"I do. I started working in a shop for a friend not long after Abe was born. Opening my own place is a dream I've had for a long time."

He smiled and the room grew even smaller. "You'll make people smile with each arrangement."

It startled her realizing how easy she found talking to Tucker. She'd just opened up to him about her dreams…. "I need to check out the upstairs," she said, heading out the door and onto the street, needing to break the moment.

Tucker followed her, of course, opting not to stand alone inside her shop while she came out onto the sidewalk. The man was like a bright, shiny penny, with his badge and buckle both glinting in the sun. And those eyes—and that warm smile spreading across his ruggedly good-looking face had Suzie's insides fluttering to life with renewed awareness.

Instantly ruining a great morning.

Tucker hadn't slept much after leaving the ranch last night. He'd gone home to his place, which was on a small piece of land just on the outskirts of Dew Drop. After moving back, he'd decided to move in closer to town. When he'd become sheriff, he found he was often barraged by calls at all times of the day and night—it was better to be closer to his office. Getting to the office quickly in an emergency situation was important to him. He'd live on the land he loved again, one day, but for now, while he'd taken the oath to serve and protect, he'd live close by. Plus, he'd felt the need to be alone at times. Especially in the beginning when nightmares kept him awake—he pushed the thought away and focused on Suzie. Helping her was the only thing that could give him some redemption from the past.

She seemed different this morning. She was upbeat and striving. He liked that. Liked it a lot that she was fighting, and that would be good for her. The woman he'd seen in the pictures didn't seem so far away right now.

"I'm sure that old shop will look like a different place when you're done. I'm pretty sure the apartment isn't livable, though. It'll be a good place to store your things until you find what you want."

"I guess we'll just go up and look," she said, starting up the steps.

Tucker followed her. The steps creaked beneath their feet but seemed sturdy. Suzie rested her hand on the banister as she went.

"Did Lester and Joyce live up here?"

"No. They had a little house over near the lake. They didn't really use this, I don't think. That's one reason I thought I might come up with you. I'm not sure if they ever came up here or if they even did anything with the stuff that had been here before they left."

She paused on the steps. "Everyone is saying they left town quickly. It sounds like they were really ready to not be tied to a business any longer."

She was a step ahead of him, and that made her almost exactly his height. He could look her straight in the eyes.

She rested her hip against the railing. "Do you think there was some other reason they left so quickly?"

"I don't know. They'd had the place up for sale for a couple of years, and I think they had almost decided just to leave anyway. Your offer came while they were packing up, so I think they didn't pause to look back."

Just as the last words were out of his mouth an ominous crack sounded and the banister Suzie was leaning against broke.

Suzie felt the board she was barely resting against give under her hip. She tried to catch her balance, arms flailing, but as the board broke there was nothing stopping her from tipping backward into open space. She was twelve feet above the ground with nothing but gravel and dirt below her.

Suddenly, a strong arm snaked around her waist and she was yanked from thin air and pulled hard against Tucker's firm chest.

"I've got you," he assured her as he swung around, throwing their momentum in the opposite direction. One moment she'd been free-falling and the next she found herself held snuggled in his arms against the brick wall of the building.

Both of them were breathing hard as she stared into his eyes. Her feet dangled beneath her and she was nose to nose, eye to eye with Tucker. Her gaze dropped to the mere inch between their lips.

"Thank you," she managed as her pulse thundered. Her mouth went dry when she met his gaze and realized he'd watched her studying his beautiful mouth.

What am I thinking! I almost plunged

*twelve feet to the ground and now I'm think-
ing about kissing Tucker. What is wrong
with me? This is so wrong.*

"No thanks required," Tucker said, taking a deep breath as if he, too, had just remembered to breathe.

She pulled away and they moved in sync,
him moving down a step, her shifting up
away from him. Even separated from him,
her skin tingled with sensation.

"That will have to be fixed," she said, as
if he didn't realize that. Silly, but it was the
first thing that popped out of her numbed
brain.

Spinning away from him and keeping
close to the building, she stared at the steps.
She moved up one step at a time to the small
landing outside the door. Key. She needed
a key.

Digging in her jeans pocket she produced
it and, with trembling fingers, inserted it
into the lock and twisted.

Tucker had followed close behind her, not

saying anything, but she knew he was as shaken as she was. She'd read it in his eyes. The tension radiated between them as she pushed open the door and stepped into the murky room.

Her thoughts were just as murky as suddenly the lights came on, and she saw Tucker had flipped the switch.

Relief washed over her, seeing that the room wasn't as full of leftover stuff as she'd feared. She moved farther inside, putting space between them.

In her mind she wanted to be grateful that he'd caught her.

But she was too shaken by the experience.

"What do you think?" Tucker's baritone radiated through the room.

Think? *That I've lost my mind.* "It, ah, isn't as bad as it could be."

"It might take a little while to get it cleaned up if you're thinking about living up here. But we could help or, if you want some walls moved around and would rather hire it done, I know a great contractor."

Suzie grabbed hold of this new topic of conversation, glad to focus on something other than how being around Tucker was affecting her. "I think we'll just store my stuff up here for now. I might decide to find a rental property instead. You know, something with a yard, so Abe could have a dog. After I get the business going, though. Maybe I can think clearer about what would be best then. Tackling the store downstairs should be my priority."

"That sounds like a plan. And you know, the ranch is your home as long as you want it. There is plenty of room. And Nana will love having you in the house with her." He was studying her, as if he were trying to read the thoughts flickering through her mind.

"But," she added quickly, "I need to have that banister repaired."

"Count it already done. I'm heading over

to the lumber company right now, and I'll have that fixed before lunch."

She wanted to say she'd get someone else, but she needed it done as soon as possible, before they began traipsing up and down with her things. Anyone could fall and she would blame herself. "Thank you again," she said. "I seem to be indebted to you over and over."

Tucker frowned. "No debt. That's all mine." With that said, he went to inspect the next room.

Suzie followed, slowly, startled that for an instant she'd forgotten what Tucker had cost her and her child. That if it wasn't for him Gordon would be alive and they wouldn't be here.

No thanks required.

That's what he'd said and it was true.

Chapter Four

Tucker called in Cody, his deputy, so he could take the morning off to get the banister rebuilt. And he needed the physical exertion—needed something to occupy his mind, but it wasn't working. He'd been thinking of nothing except holding Suzie in his arms all morning.

What a jerk he'd been. He'd rescued her, and then instantly his pulse had ramped up and he'd been looking at her as if she was his long-lost love. And she'd seen it, too.

He slammed the hammer to the nail with enough force to test the foundation poles holding the stairs in the air. He needed the exertion that working with his hands would provide. Riding his horse across the ranch would have been his number one choice to exert his pent-up frustrations—as far away from Suzie Kent as he could get. But she needed the banister and despite knowing that she was just inside the building, it was where he needed to be.

His reaction to her had stunned him. She was the wife of the man he owed his life to. *Widow.* His brain corrected. *And free to find a new love.*

That his thoughts had even hinted at going there angered him. He owed Gordon his life, and he owed Gordon's widow and child his support to help them maneuver through the wreckage he'd caused in their lives. But to think about her in terms of a love interest—nope, she was way out of bounds to him.

And yet there was no denying that he was attracted to her. *Or that she's the kind of woman I've been looking for all of my life.*

But there was no chance for there to ever be anything between them—and he had no right even thinking about it. Feeling cornered, he placed another nail in the base of the banister railing and then moved up the steps to hammer in the next one. Six more to go, and not near enough to get rid of the anger fighting inside of him.

He was a man who took action. He'd had to watch his mother die of cancer when he was fourteen and there had been nothing he could do about it. He'd sworn then that he'd make a difference in the lives of others and the marines had drawn him. He'd wanted to make a difference in the world. Time after time he'd pulled his men back from death, or as many as he possibly could. He'd been able to make a difference in their lives and those of their families. Unlike his own. Cancer was a war that many were able to defeat, but his mom had not been one of them.

He'd never thought about what watching

helplessly as one of his men gave his life for him would cost—not only the soldier's family, but him.

He didn't like it. He couldn't control it. But he was going to fix it. And being attracted to Gordon's widow was the ultimate betrayal of his friend. Tucker had been sixteen when that first group of boys had started filtering in, and Gordon had been two years younger when he'd come to Sunrise Ranch the year it opened. Tucker and Gordon had hit it off instantly.

It had been a surprise when Gordon had ended up in his marine unit. They'd celebrated, not realizing that it would come down to one of them living and the other dying.

Tucker closed his eyes, thinking about it. Kenny Chesney's "Who You'd Be Today" played through his mind, as it did so many times when he thought about Gordon and the others who didn't come home.

"Woo-hoo, Tucker!"

At the excited singsong holler he opened his eyes, to see Mabel Tilsby, owner of the Dew Drop Inn, weaving her way across the street toward him. A tall, stout woman, she had the heart of a missionary, and that was a good thing because Tucker was pretty sure an angry Mabel could take care of herself.

"You are doing one great job," she said, drawing to a halt at the bottom of the stairs. "These old stairs have been here since the beginning of time, and they did need repairing." Hands on hips, she grinned up at him. "I was out front this morning when I saw them break. Thank goodness you were there to save our new resident!"

He glanced across the street and saw that she had a straight shot of the stairs from her front door. He groaned inwardly knowing exactly what Mabel saw—him holding Suzie in his arms longer than necessary.

"Yeah, I should have checked these out a long time ago when I was making my rounds at night." It was known by everyone that he still walked the square on foot each evening to make sure everything was secure. An odd thing, some might say, since Dew Drop was such a small place and the crime rate was low, but even small towns had problems. And it was his job to make sure his tiny hometown stayed safe.

"You can't fix everything, even though you think you're our superhero sheriff," she said jovially.

Tucker had always liked Mabel. She was a tower of a woman, and with her big-boned frame could almost have been a linebacker if she'd been born a male. His mother used to say that a tall person needed bigger feet to balance out their height, and that Mabel needed her larger size to balance out her large and loving personality. He believed it, too. Mabel would just as soon pick you up and hug you in half as shake your hand.

"Nope, but I can try." He grinned back at her.

She waved him off. "You got it honestly

from both sides of your family. I'm going to go inside and introduce myself. Have to tell that girl how much I loved Gordon. I always smile thinking about that boy. Ta-ta for now."

And she was gone, disappearing inside the shop. Suzie would hear a lot of good stories about Gordon from Mabel since he'd worked for her as a bellboy whenever she needed help.

Tucker went back to hammering.

And his mind went straight back to thinking about how Suzie Kent had felt in his arms.

Though the previous owners had left the shop in decent shape, such as it was, there were spiderwebs and dust in the nooks and crannies. She had busied herself cleaning, getting it ready to paint. Paint worked wonders, and she was counting on it for the store.

The thump of the hammer outside was a

continual reminder that she'd made a fool of herself by looking up into Tucker McDermott's eyes like a love-starved widow. How humiliating that cliché was. The more she thought about it, the worse it got.

In addition came the guilt that she'd done so with Tucker. It would have been bad with anyone—but Tucker? It was awful. Guilt engulfed her. And even if Tucker hadn't been the man she blamed for Gordon's death, he was in law enforcement. She could never again risk falling for a man who worked in the line of fire. And yet, she couldn't deny that the man affected her in startling ways.

When a large woman came barreling through the open door, Suzie was more than ready for company.

"Hello, hello. I'm Mabel Tilsby, owner of the Dew Drop Inn—hope you don't mind me dropping in on you." She grinned, taking Suzie's hands in hers for an extended moment.

"Not at all. I'm glad to meet you."

"I have to tell you that I loved your husband. That Gordon was a good young man. He'd had a rough life, but he came right to this town and brightened it with his smile and good humor. Do you know he rescued me that first summer?"

Suzie couldn't speak at first, startled by Mabel's declaration. Of course there would be stories of Gordon. This was his home. She was touched and then remembered him mentioning the owner of the hotel. "He mentioned you," she said, smiling. "I remember he said you were a wonderful lady."

That made Mabel blush, her eyes misted. "That boy always was a sweetheart. And just look at you. So beautiful and young. I know he must have loved you very much."

It was Suzie's turn to get misty-eyed. She nodded. "He did."

"Well." Mabel heaved a deep breath in then expelled it. "He'd be happy you've come home and brought his boy. You've got a lot of life ahead of you. He'd want you to move forward—or in his case he'd want you to plow forward like he always did."

Suzie laughed at that. "Yes, he did move at a fast pace."

Mabel nodded and then studied the shop.

"This old place needed new blood in it. So, what do you think?"

Suzie had been destroying a large web in the upper corner of the ceiling when Mabel burst into the building. She smiled. "Minus all the spiders, let's just say I'm counting on paint to make a whole new world in here. Paint and flowers."

"It is ancient."

"Yes, but serviceable, and that's what counts. As long as I get some orders for flowers when I open the doors."

"You'll get them. And you have such a handsome handyman outside. That has to be a plus."

"He's not my handyman. He's just—" *What? Fixing your banister. Being your handyman.* "It broke while we were going up to look upstairs. Mr. McDermott and Rowdy are going to come in a little while and help Tucker unload my moving truck and store my things up there for now. I think some of the boys are coming, too, and we didn't want anyone getting hurt."

"I understand. Falling from those stairs wouldn't be good. I saw you almost tumble off this morning. Thank goodness our fabulous sheriff was there. I almost screamed from the steps of the Inn when I realized what was happening. But then, just like that, you were in his arms and safe." Mabel sighed as she finished and her eyes got dreamy—it was enough to make Suzie worry.

And she felt the heat of a blush race over her as though she'd just been doused in warm cherry juice. "So, come over here and see what you think about the colors I'm going to paint the shop," she said, changing the subject.

She popped the top of the can of paint in a soft buttery-yellow that she'd picked up at the lumber store.

"Oh, I like that," Mabel gushed enthusiastically.

Suzie was learning that everything Mabel did was with enthusiasm. It was kind of contagious.

"I think it's a happy color. It'll make a perky background for the flowers."

"I most certainly agree, hon. I'll go tell the girls and we'll have a full-scale painting party. How does that sound? All you have to do is tell us where you want it, and we can slap it up there in no time. Matter of fact, have you had lunch?"

Suzie looked at her watch and was startled to see that it was past noon. "No, but—"

"Nope, no buts allowed. You're coming with me. Seal up that can and let's go. When were you planning on painting?"

She found herself swept out of the shop and managed to squeeze in "I'll be back" to Tucker—not that it was any of his business, but he was working on her stairs and he would be lugging her furniture up them before too much later. He nodded that he heard and went back to hammering. They headed down the street with Mabel talking nonstop.

"That man sure looks good swinging a hammer," Mabel sighed, elbowing her in the ribs before continuing to talk about paint. Before they made it to the café she'd learned that mission trips and fixing things up for folks in need were high priorities for Mabel. It hit Suzie that she'd just been added to the top of Mabel's folks-in-need list.

She'd become a mission project.

Suzie wasn't sure how to take that. She took care of herself, or had been trying to. But as they took their seats in the diner and were joined by Ms. Jo, the owner, who was Mabel's buddy and also Nana's, Suzie had the oddest sensation that she'd been embraced. Embraced by a town. Being helped just came with the deal.

Gordon would be happy. The knowledge echoed through her heart and she had to fight off a sudden wave of emotion.

Her being happy again would have been what he'd wanted. It felt good knowing that, here in Dew Drop, it was a possibility.

Despite Tucker and her conflicting emotions.

Later that afternoon, after an already full day, Tucker watched his dad back the moving truck up to the newly renovated stairs. Just as Randolph and Morgan climbed from the truck, Rowdy pulled in beside them with a truck full of the older boys, including Abe.

"Hey, guys," he said. "Thanks for coming to help."

"Sure thing," Jake said. He was new at the ranch, having taken one of the vacant spots left when Joseph and Wes, two of the older boys, headed off to college. Jake didn't speak much about what he'd been through before he came to them, but he'd had it rough, even lived on the streets for a while. The kid had taken to the ranch as if he'd been born a cowboy, always ready to mount up and herd cattle or pitch in where needed.

Tucker noticed Abe stood back from the group and didn't look pleased to be here.

"So, did you check out the apartment up there?" Randolph asked, striding over to stand beside him.

Morgan nodded toward Tucker's handyman project. "Hopefully, it's more stable now."

"Yeah," Rowdy said, grabbing the banister and tugging to test its sturdiness. "Did they teach you to be a carpenter in the marines? Because I don't remember you ever building anything before now. You sure this thing will hold us?"

"Oh, it'll hold," Tucker assured them,

heading toward the moving van instead of thinking about that banister breaking and him pulling Suzie into his arms.

As if on cue, Suzie stepped out of the office right at that moment, and she smiled— not at him but at everyone else.

"Thank you all for coming," she said, warmly. She'd been painting already, and there was a splotch of yellow paint on her jaw. He busied himself opening the cargo doors as the boys gathered around.

"Abe, how was school today?" she asked.

"All right, I guess," Abe answered, his voice flat.

"Well, good. I'm glad it was all right," she said and Tucker liked that she was trying to be positive.

"He's gonna ride a horse when we get back to the ranch. Isn't that right?" Jake prompted.

Though he remained silent, Abe's scowl was a definite "no."

"Come on," Tony encouraged. "You said you would."

"Yeah, I heard you," Caleb challenged.

"Fine, whatever. I'll ride," Abe agreed, but he continued to frown.

Jake grinned. "That's what I'm talking about!"

"Abe, that's wonderful," Suzie said. "I might try riding sometime, too."

Tucker knew she was putting on a front but was probably worried about the obvious mood Abe was in.

"We've got extremely gentle horses for beginners," Randolph told her. "So anytime you want to ride, you tell us or Walter Pepper, our horse foreman, and we'll get you on one and make sure you have a good time."

Tucker opened the doors wide and noted that it wasn't crammed full. "Suzie, if you'll tell us how you want this done we'll get it finished in no time. Won't we, boys?"

Within minutes it was settled and the unloading began. Tucker and Rowdy took control of getting the couch up the stairs, which proved tricky. The task of getting it through the door and across the small landing was precarious.

"Don't fall over the banister," Suzie warned.

Tucker's position on the end tested his handyman skills to the limit as he had to bend backward over the banister while holding the couch, and then push it through the door. He hiked a brow at Suzie from his dangerous position.

"Just testing my double-reinforced banister for you, ma'am," he drawled, bringing a smile to her worried expression as he moved past her through the doorway.

"So that was what all the hammering was about." She laughed. "I have never in all my life heard that much hammering at one time."

"Yup, it'll hold," he grunted, pushing through and into the building as Rowdy pulled on the other end of the couch. He didn't tell her that there were enough nails in that banister to reinforce Texas, if need be. And still, he hadn't gotten rid of the frustrations that holding her in his arms had generated.

They managed to test the banister a few more times bringing up a chest of drawers and her kitchen table. He figured if there had been a kitchen sink to haul up, that that might have done it in. But, fortunately, there wasn't one. The boys were over in a corner trying on old hats they found in a box of Joyce and Lester's leftover stuff. Everyone was watching them. Even Abe put on an old derby hat and almost smiled. Almost—it was a Kodak moment. If they'd had a camera, which they didn't. Of course she did have her cell phone camera, but Abe would have been mortified if she'd asked to take his picture.

"Hey up there, I brought y'all some pie."

Ms. Jo's holler from downstairs had them all reacting. No one turned down her pie.

The boys sounded like a cattle stampede tromping down the stairs.

Tucker held back, watching the rush from the top of the landing. Tiny Ms. Jo, with her cap of dark gray hair, had set a tray on the empty floor of the moving van and smiled happily as she began dishing out the pie onto paper plates. From his vantage point, he could see the wonder on Suzie's face as she watched Ms. Jo's hospitality.

He would have to give Ms. Jo a hug later for knowing the perfect way to end the day. Like his nana, she had a knack for making folks smile.

The fact that it was Suzie's smile he was seeing, as she savored the taste of Ms. Jo's Triple Chocolate Wonder pie, made watching all the sweeter to him.

Chapter Five

It had been an eventful day, from beginning till evening, but Suzie's spirits were humming with energy as she arrived back at the ranch. Maybe it was a sugar high from Ms. Jo's amazing chocolate pie but Suzie knew that was just part of it. It had just been an amazing day—despite the shaky moment of being in Tucker's arms, the rest had been wonderful.

"Suzie, come up and join us."

She hadn't even realized Nana was on the porch and she wasn't alone. "Sure," she called, heading that way. Jolie was there and so was another woman, a stunning blonde.

It turned out to be Lucy, Rowdy's fiancée, the talented artist. Suzie suddenly felt like a plain, ordinary female in the presence of these two accomplished women. After her mother had grown ill, Suzie had been unable to finish high school, much less move on to any kind of greatness. Her biggest claim to fame was Abe, and she'd managed to mess that up, too, by not holding it together after losing Gordon.

"Sit down and let me pour you a glass of tea," Nana said, after introducing Lucy.

"Thank you," Suzie said, feeling exhausted all of a sudden. She sank onto a brown wicker chair with red cushions and met the smiles of Jolie and Lucy with a forced one of her own. "It's been a long day," she explained. "How did Abe do at school?"

"Fair," Jolie said, honestly. "He was quiet, frowned a lot, but not disrespectful. He's taking it all in right now, figuring out what he thinks about everything."

"Thank you for working with him."

Jolie's Julia Roberts smile was wide and encouraging. "I love it. Working with these boys is a joy. Lucy teaches them art for me, and they love her, too."

"Yes, that's what I hear. I saw some of the artwork yesterday when Tucker showed the school to me."

Lucy's eyes twinkled. "I had no idea when I moved here that I was going to fall in love and get to work with these boys."

"I can see how it would be rewarding. And I loved the mural with the young cowboys."

"Me, too! I've always been partial to roads and landscapes but then I came here and now, all I want to paint are paintings that showcase the boys and Rowdy branding calves. She hiked a brow above her gorgeous eyes—everything about the pint-size artist was beautiful. "It's been a wonderful blessing coming here, in more ways than one."

"I can't wait to see more of your work. It sounds amazing."

Nana paused before sipping her tea. "We have a weekly art class at her place on Tuesday nights. You should come—although, that evening we're working on decorations for Lucy and Rowdy's wedding in two weeks."

"Um, I've never painted anything other than walls of a room. But I would love to help with the decorations."

"Sure, that would be great. We could use your help on the silk flowers. And no worries about the painting," Jolie said, pointing at Lucy. "That woman there can make you feel like an artist even if you paint stick art. She has a gift."

"I'm so excited you'll come help," Lucy said. "But you have to promise that when I get back from our honeymoon you'll come to art night. It's our ladies' night out. We're a wild bunch." They all laughed at that, and Suzie couldn't help but look forward to being around them more.

"I'll come," she said. "It sounds like too much fun to pass up."

"Wonderful." Lucy nodded toward Rowdy in the arena with a horse and one of the boys. "I love watching that man work with a horse."

"He looks like a good instructor," Suzie said, seeing his patience.

"He loves it." Lucy smiled as she watched her fiancé.

"All of them do," Nana added. "My grandsons had as much love bestowed on them by my daughter-in-law as any kids could ever have. In the short time that Lydia got to be here with her boys, she lavished them with an abundance of love and nurturing. Never saw a woman with as big a heart as she had. So my grandsons know what these other boys are missing in their lives. Most of them were abandoned, either physically or emotionally, and never understood what a real family was like." Nana smiled gently at her. "Unlike your son. Abe has obviously been very loved. Like my grandsons, his parent died, forcing his parent to leave. But the parents of the boys who come to the ranch—their parents willingly gave them up."

Suzie's heart clutched in her chest as if someone had stomped hard on the brakes. She could only nod. A revelation spiked across her thoughts.

"What I'm trying to say is that there is no better place for Abe to recover than here, with the leadership of these strong men Lydia's sons have become."

"And we came together specifically this afternoon to let you know that we want to be here as a support group for you," Jolie added. "None of us have walked in your shoes, but we are here for you. In any way you need us."

"That's right," Nana agreed. "Mabel called

to tell us about the painting party tomorrow at your shop. How does that sound?"

Shocked, Suzie took a shaky breath and looked about the group. "Thank you. That means a lot to me." She teared up, looking at their smiling faces she could barely speak. "All of it does."

"That's what friends are for," Nana said. "You just relax and this is all going to work out."

"That's right. Abe will get through this," Jolie continued. "All of these boys have lost both of their parents, whether through the courts or through death. When they come to us they are boys who will never be sent back to their birth parents, the majority anyway, and because of that, they need nurturing men and women involved in their lives. If you ever feel led to volunteer or just want to help out, we would love it. Just so you know."

The idea appealed to her, even though she

had a business to get up and running. "After I get situated I'd love to get involved."

"You'll be blessed by it, I can promise," Lucy said, her eyes twinkling.

"I'm sure I will." Suzie nodded, following Lucy's gaze as it went back to Rowdy and the little boy.

"There's a lot to learn from these boys," Jolie added. "Their circumstances could have made them victims but they're survivors. They didn't have a choice about the lot they were given, but they do have a choice how they react to it."

Suzie agreed with her, but Nana's words echoed through her mind. *Like my grandsons, his parent died, forcing his parent to leave. But the parents of the boys who come to the ranch—their parents willingly gave them up.*

Suddenly fighting back more tears, it hit Suzie and she knew Nana had been wrong. Abe's dad had dived in front of Tucker McDermott of his own free will. He'd chosen to let Tucker live and his son grow up without a dad. That was the lot Abe had been given, and he wasn't handling it well.

Abe's father had, in a way, willingly abandoned him, just as these other boys' parents had done.

And she believed that knowledge was at the root of Abe's problems.

It was certainly at the root of hers. Because Gordon had abandoned her, too...and she hadn't handled it well.

Had she allowed herself to be a victim?

Stunned, Suzie hid her emotions and took a sip of her drink, pretending everything was fine.

But the revelation was hard to take.

Tucker had peeked in the flower shop window every night for a week as he made his rounds and the inside had begun to look like a different place.

He had been proud of the way Mabel, Ms. Jo, Nana, Jolie and Lucy had jumped in to help Suzie. The second day she'd shown up to open the shop they'd all come running— all but Jolie, who'd had to work. She'd joined them as soon as school was out and they'd had the shop painted in no time.

He'd thought of every excuse in the book to come see the progress in the daytime and had to force himself not to do it. Suzie needed time to adjust without him trailing her about.

But he'd been keeping up. At a distance.

He needed to talk to her today, though. The door was open and he walked into the freshly painted room. The soft buttery tone was a far sight from the drab place he'd looked at the first of the week.

"Suzie, are you here?" He could hear humming and headed that way. "Suzie," he said again as he stepped through the archway into the back room. Suzie stood at the back wall, her back to him as she sang softly while she painted one of the cabinets deep red.

"Suzie," he said, louder, hoping not to startle her—failing when she screamed and spun around. Disaster happened quickly as her elbow caught the can of paint and sent it flying.

Tucker tried to grab it but succeeded only in stepping into the line of fire. The can hit his outstretched hands and launched the contents straight at him. It got his tan uniform with a direct hit. He had red paint dripping from his badge to his boots.

"Oh, my stars!" Suzie squealed. Only seconds had passed since he'd startled her. "What have I done?"

Feeling bad for her and berating himself for walking in and scaring her, he shrugged. "You didn't do anything. I know not to walk up on someone like that."

She thought about that for a blink of an eye. "True. You do. But look at you." Hurrying to a roll of paper towels she came over and started blotting him down, going for his radio and phone first. The rest was hopeless.

"It's water-based paint, but still, your uniform is ruined."

"I have more," Tucker assured her. He couldn't have cared less about the uniform as he stared at Suzie, flashing back to the day on the stairs.

Her hair had fallen loose from behind her ear and swung free as she tried unsuccessfully to dab the paint from him. A few strands of pale blond hair now had red paint on them, too.

Instinctively he reached for those strands and rubbed the paint off with his fingers. Her brows dipped and suddenly her concerned eyes flared.

She stepped away from him.

"Water. You should go put water on this now. I have a hose hooked up outside by the back door for cleaning paint rollers and pans."

"I'll do that. Then I'll help clean up the floor."

Suzie's look of horror at what she'd done

turned more alarmed. "You will not clean up the floor. I'm the one who doused you. I'll take care of this. Hurry, you might be able to save your uniform if you wet it down before it dries."

Striding across the room and out the door before he made a complete idiot out of himself, Tucker took his radio and cell phone off and set them on a small table by the back door.

Finding the hose, he twisted the knob and drenched himself with the water. He needed something to snap him out of the continual lapses of bad judgment on his part where Suzie was concerned.

Red paint, even water-based, was not the easiest thing to wash away. It looked as though he'd cut an artery or something as the paint ran off him and pooled in the scraggly grass and dirt.

After a few minutes Suzie came out the back door carrying a towel covered in the crimson paint.

"How's it looking in there?" he asked, feeling like a drowned rat. Soaking himself down might not have been the best solution to this situation.

She bit her lip and he could tell she was fighting back a smile. "Better than it looks like it's going out here."

He cocked his head. "That's a plus. I'd hate for you to continually have to tell people what the big red stain on the floor is."

She smiled. "That would get old after a while. Folks might start thinking I'd committed some terrible crime, Sheriff."

"Good thing most of it got on me."

She bit her lip, holding back a smile, and held the towel out. "You look terrible."

"Thanks." He laughed. "All I can say is you have great reflexes and on-target instincts. If someone tried to sneak up on you they'd be in for a surprise, even if you weren't wielding a can of paint."

Her eyes twinkled as she shook her head. "I'm glad I have something going for me.

Could you point that water this way and let me rinse this out?"

"Why, I'd be happy to do that," he teased, and swung the hose toward her. It hit the towel, and the force of the water splattered red paint all over her, instantly making her look as though she had the measles.

She gasped.

Tucker did, too, shocked at what he'd done.

They stared at each other, pink and red spots everywhere—and burst into laughter.

"I promise you I did not do that in retaliation," he said, between chuckles.

"I wouldn't blame you if you did."

She was so beautiful. Without thinking he gently wiped a spot from her cheek.

Her laughter died. She swayed toward him and then suddenly backed away. "I…I'm here for Abe," she snapped, shaking her head, looking confused.

"I'm just here to help. That's all."

She didn't look as if she believed him and that was his own fault. How many times had he grabbed her or touched her? Too many.

"You have nothing to fear from me," he said. Moving to the faucet he turned the water off, stopping the flood around them. "I'd better head home and change."

He picked up his phone and radio, and started toward the side of the building, his boots sloshing and his jeans dragging. He climbed into his SUV, not even caring that he was dripping murky pink water all over everything.

He'd almost kissed Suzie again—no wonder she was leery of him. They'd been laughing and relaxed, a good thing in the dynamics of their working together to help Abe.

But no, he'd lost his head.

He was a man who never lost his head. He was cool under fire and clear thinking through the worst of times. And yet, around Suzie he didn't think.

His phone rang before he backed out of

the parking lot. Glancing at the name, he punched the talk button. "Hey, Dad," he said, his voice calm, giving away none of the turmoil eating at him.

"Tucker, we have a situation out here."

Chapter Six

She should have just stayed inside earlier. But no, she'd had to go check on Tucker. Had to go outside after him and just look what had happened. Suzie's face was hot as she stormed back into the shop, snatched a towel up and swiped the last puddle of paint off the wooden floor.

She'd behaved like a fool.

Part of it had been due to the fact that she'd decided she was being a simpering victim when it came to dealing with being a widow.

She'd been so angry for the past two years. Angry at God. Angry at the military.

At Gordon. And especially at Tucker. And then this situation with Abe had started, and she'd gotten angrier.

She was a mess and she knew it. She had things to work through, things to change about herself. And the one thing she didn't need complicating matters was this attraction—there, she'd said it. There was an attraction between her and Tucker that had no place there. Hopefully he understood that.

Hopefully she'd made that perfectly clear just now.

The door to the shop opened and Tucker poked his head inside. "Suzie, we have a problem at the school. It's going to be all right, but I need you to come with me."

Her heart dropped to her knees. "What's happened?" she asked, rushing across the room, tossing the rag to the floor as she went.

"Abe and Jake got into a fight."

"Are they hurt?"

"They're fine. Lock up. I'll drive."

Nodding, full of questions and turmoil, she hurried to grab her purse, locking both the back door and the front door. Still dripping wet, Tucker held the door of the SUV open for her then trudged around to his side. He was so wet he looked uncomfortable as they buckled up and he drove toward the ranch.

"A fight?" she said. "With Jake. I thought they had been becoming friends."

"Boys fight sometimes, Suzie. This could be nothing."

The miles to the ranch seemed endless when, in reality, it took twenty minutes to travel the country roads. In the city it could have taken hours in traffic, and she kept reminding herself of this as she watched the pastures flow by.

Tucker pulled up to the ranch office and they got out. She waited for him to lead the way, aware that they were being watched from the arena by young eyes. His boots squished as he strode across the wooden porch and held the door open for her.

Though he wasn't dripping now, he looked terrible, his tan uniform shirt had turned a marbled crimson and pink, and his jeans were not much different. "I'm so sorry," she said, everything that had happened forgotten other than he was dealing with her problems looking like this and it was her fault.

"It'll be fine," he said. "We're here to find out what's going on between Abe and Jake, and to help them resolve the issue."

"Thank you" was all she could say as she followed him inside and through the door to one of the offices.

Jake and Abe sat in the rich brown leather chairs in front of the large desk, each one of them had a cut lip and an ice pack. Dirt and sprigs of grass clung to their clothing and their rumpled hair.

Randolph sat behind the desk looking serious, but not overly upset. Unlike Suzie, whose insides were curled up in a ball. Her hands were shaking, she was so upset. How many other times had she been called to the school office over the past year for Abe's problems? She had hoped that it would change here.

But there he sat looking as if he didn't care about anything.

Randolph stood. "Suzie, why don't you come sit here, in my chair?" He gave her a reassuring smile and she did as he asked because her knees were too wobbly to hold her.

"Thank you," she said, walking around the desk and taking the seat. "What happened?"

Neither of the boys would look at her.

"We don't know for sure, since they aren't talking," Randolph answered. "Jolie found them taking swings at each other behind the school when she was leaving—about thirty minutes after school had been dismissed for the day."

"You fellas want to tell us what's going

on?" Tucker asked, drawing sullen looks from both.

"What happened to you?" Jake asked, taking in Tucker's appearance.

"It's a long story, but it's your story I'm interested in right now. Not mine."

Jake looked almost embarrassed as his gaze shifted away and he firmly clamped his lips together.

"Abe," Tucker said. "How about you? Want to tell us what's going on between the two of you?"

Suzie studied her son. "Abe, answer Sheriff Tucker."

He shot her a sullen look.

Tucker gave her a hint of a smile. "I do have on my uniform—or what remains of my uniform," he said, his smile lifting to his eyes. "But, so you boys will know, I'm not here as the sheriff. I'm here as a member of this family. Dad called me because we have a family situation and we need to work together to get it resolved."

"That's right," Randolph added, patting Suzie on the shoulder. "Both of you boys are new here, and this is how we do things. We mess up as a family and we resolve issues as a family. I don't know what's going on between the two of you and if you're not going to tell me, I'm not going to force you. Sometimes a man has a reason for keeping silent. But if either of you need to speak in private there is always that option."

Tucker had leaned a shoulder against the wall and looked very relaxed now, watching the boys. Suzie realized that he might appear completely at ease, but he was taking in everything. "We're all here to talk about anything bothering either one of you," he said.

Suzie liked how they emphasized family. Nana had done that same thing.

"So, if you have nothing to say, then head on back outside," Randolph said. Both boys stood up as if they'd been shot from a cannon. Jake looked relieved and Abe looked a little disbelieving. After all, at his previous school he would have received detention. Here he was being set free with no penalties. Suzie was about to say something about that. She was worried about Abe but he had to know there were consequences for his actions. Even among family. They were almost to the door when Randolph halted them.

"There is one more thing, fellas." They turned toward him, both only a step from exiting. "I don't like fighting. A man has to do what a man has to do sometimes. But for the most part a fight is avoidable. There are other ways to resolve your differences. Talking about it is usually the best way. So, to give you the opportunity to resolve this issue on your own, you're both assigned two weeks of mucking out the horse stables every evening together."

There was no hiding their dismay. "Yes, sir," Jake said, but Abe only shrugged.

"You can go now. I'll let Pepper know

there won't be a rotation for a couple of weeks." After they had gone and Tucker pulled the door closed, Randolph patted her shoulder again.

"It happens. Boys fight, so don't get too upset. Working together will either push whatever's bugging them to the surface and it'll come out or they'll resolve the issue and move forward."

Tucker grinned. "It's amazing how much life-changing bonding can go on when you're cleaning out stalls on a regular basis."

Suzie wouldn't know, having never done it, but it sounded like something she wouldn't enjoy at all. "I'll take your word for it."

Randolph looked from Tucker to Suzie and she was suddenly reminded that though not as bad as Tucker's, her clothing wasn't much better off. "Now, mind explaining what happened to y'all?"

Tucker chuckled. "I'll just offer this piece

of advice, Dad. Never surprise a woman standing near a can of paint."

Randolph laughed. "Sounds like a great piece of advice. Thanks."

Tucker winked at her and despite all that had happened, she laughed.

After they left the office Tucker closed the door of his SUV and looked across at Suzie. "I'd like to drive over to the school before I take you back to town, if that's okay with you."

"Of course, do whatever you need to do. What are you looking for?"

"Something started that altercation between Abe and Jake and I don't like that they aren't talking. I want to look around where the fight happened."

"Sure, that sounds like a good idea. I know you have to be miserable in those clothes. I am so sorry."

"It's fine. They're drying. A few more minutes won't matter anyway."

He drove across the pasture and pulled around behind the school where Jolie had found them fighting. He would talk to her himself when he saw her. "I know I said I wasn't here as the sheriff and I meant that. But still, we need to get to the bottom of this even if the boys choose not to tell us what was going on."

"I agree."

Tucker walked over and surveyed the area. It was clear where the fight had ended, because the grass and dirt were disturbed. Tucker stood beside the area and surveyed the school and the grounds. Noticing something in the bushes he walked over and moved a limb out of the way as he reached for the fluorescent orange can.

"What is it?" Suzie came to stand beside him.

Looking up at her he frowned. "A can of spray paint."

Instantly, her face fell. "No."

"What do you think?" he asked, having his own suspicions but wanting her thoughts first.

"Abe got in trouble vandalizing property with spray paint."

He nodded. "So did Jake."

Her brows crinkled and her expression grew stormy. "I just don't know, Tucker. I don't get it. Abe can be mad, he can be furious and hurt about what happened to his dad, but I don't understand destroying people's property. I just don't understand it. As soon as I get back to the ranch I'm going to have a long talk with my son. This is ridiculous."

"As his parent, that's your prerogative. But my opinion is to hold off for a little while. See if the boys come clean about what they were doing. And of course there is the possibility this doesn't belong to them."

"You don't really believe that, do you?"

He shook his head. "No. But in my line of duty, a man is innocent until proven guilty or he confesses. And Dad is trying to let them work through this together."

"Okay. He doesn't listen to me right now anyway, so I'll go along with you and Randolph and we'll see if they step up."

"Good. I'm disappointed in both of them, but the opportunity to fess up gives them the opportunity to redeem themselves. Which is Dad's hope."

"Then we'll go with that. Thank you, Tucker."

He tugged his hat snugger on his head. "No thanks needed." He started back toward the vehicle. "Okay, now it's time for me to find some dry clothes."

"Yes, better hurry before some new disaster arises."

"Agreed. Let's roll."

"Are you all right?" Rowdy asked the morning after the paint fiasco. "You're not looking so good."

The donkeys had escaped again and

the men were loading them into a trailer bound for Sunrise Ranch, where they would remain until their escape route was discovered.

"See, there you go hurting your big brother's feelings," Tucker said, teasing his way out of this conversation. "Just because you got the real looks of the family, you don't have to always rub it in."

Rowdy stared at him, knowing full well what he was doing. "Hey, I can't help it if I got the looks. At least you got the height."

"True, there is that." Tucker chuckled as the last of the donkeys stepped up into the trailer with the enthusiasm of a kid going to the dentist. At six-two he was just a hair taller than his brother.

"There you go, Tucker. Our work here is done." Tony grinned and pushed the ever-present lock of thick black hair out of his left eye. Tony would be taking his driving test in a week and they were giving him every opportunity to practice. "Thanks, Tony, couldn't have done it without you."

"I know." He grinned. "Hey, did you hear Wes is riding bulls?"

Wes had just turned eighteen, as had Joseph. Both had been raised on the ranch and were now in their first semester at Sam Houston. "He always did want to do that," Tucker said, not surprised.

Rowdy closed the trailer gate. "He's good. Got on the team as a walk-on, but hasn't told anyone till now."

Bull riding was the one rodeo sport their dad, Randolph, didn't allow at Sunrise Ranch. Tucker and Rowdy both knew you didn't just walk on to a college team without prior experience. No one had talked about it much last year, but they'd all suspected that Wes had been riding on weekends and not saying anything about it. This was proof. Randolph didn't allow bull riding *on* the ranch, but he'd never specifically forbidden it away from the ranch. It was that gray area

Wes had operated under. Just as Tucker and his brothers had growing up, the older boys had use of trucks and the rights to spend time off the ranch with their friends.

Tucker knew there had been something inside of Wes that drew him to bull riding. Though good-natured, he had been pulled to anything that had an edge to it. Tucker had been a lot like that as a kid. But instead of bulls, he'd been fascinated by the marines. Gordon had been the same way. When a man truly wanted to do something, there was no stopping him. Tucker recognized that in Wes and hadn't butted in when he'd suspected he was riding.

"He'll be all right," he said. "If he rides a bull half as well as he rides a horse, then he'll be at the National Finals Rodeo before you know it. I better get to town—if y'all can haul them to the ranch that'd be great. We'll get the boys and go over to Chili's this weekend to ride his fence line. We've got to find out how these misfits are getting out before someone gets hurt."

"Will do," Rowdy said. He watched Tony head toward the driver's seat of the truck. "That boy can't get enough of driving," he added. "If Chili spent a little more time ranching instead of sitting in town whittling, these donkeys wouldn't be such troublemakers."

"That's the truth." Tucker started toward his SUV, remembering the painful walk to it the last time they'd dealt with the donkeys. He was thankful an ice pack had fixed him up. He'd made certain to stay out of their way this time.

"You sure you're all right?"

Tucker knew what Rowdy was asking. Rowdy knew the weight of his guilt. Anyone who knew him, and understood the code that drove him, knew that he'd taken full responsibility for their friend—their *brother's*—death.

"I'm making it," he offered. "I can't let them down, Rowdy."

Rowdy's eyes narrowed. "You won't, bro. You've never let anyone down. Gordon was a marine, same as you. If you hadn't been shot, you would have been the one to draw fire—you'd done it before. Gordon was no different and you know that. You have to accept it."

"Yeah, well, that doesn't make it any easier. I have to do right by his son. By his wife."

Rowdy clamped him on the shoulder. "You will."

"Thanks for the confidence. Tony didn't happen to say anything about the fight between Abe and Jake this morning, did he?"

"Nope. If any of them know what happened between those two, they aren't saying."

"Yeah, that's what I figured. Talk to you later. Duty calls."

He was almost to his truck when Rowdy's words stopped him. "You like her, don't you?"

Tucker hadn't expected Rowdy's question. He scowled. "You better go. Your driver will leave you."

"Yup. Just what I thought."

"Now, Rowdy, don't get any ideas. Yeah, I like her. But nothing could ever come of that. Nothing."

"And why not?"

"That's a crazy question. You know why. She would never be able to look at me and not think of Gordon. And as much as I like to look at her, he is always on my mind, too."

"That's some tough stuff," Rowdy said. "I don't like it, but I get it. And if that's how you really feel then I would be extra careful. Don't get in too deep."

"Hey, you don't need to be worrying about me. You have a wedding in two weeks."

Rowdy grinned. "Don't worry, Tuck.

Thinking about that beautiful lady walking down the aisle wins every time."

Tucker slapped his brother on the back as he turned to head toward his truck.

Don't get in too deep. Tucker thought about that advice for the rest of the day. He hoped it was that easy, but he had a bad feeling he'd already dug a hole he was going to have a hard time crawling out of.

Chapter Seven

Breakfast in the chow hall was just getting finished when Suzie saw the trailer filled with renegade donkeys wheel into the yard. Tony was driving and waved as he and Rowdy passed by.

Suzie walked to her car, watching as he backed the trailer up to the unloading pen at the far end of the arena. The beasts were staying here, it seemed.

Seconds later, the boys came flooding out of the chow hall to see what was going on. Obviously they'd known Tony had gone to help Rowdy load the animals, since he wasn't at breakfast. She had helped in the kitchen today, reluctant about leaving Abe. He'd remained closemouthed about the fight and had hardly spoken at all last night.

Whoops went up as the boys gathered around the trailer, watching Tony herd the donkeys into the pen. Abe jumped onto the fence, his excitement evident from the way he scrambled to the top to lean out and watch the animals. Rowdy had emerged from the passenger's side of the truck and looked as if he was joking around with the guys.

She wondered where Tucker was. She assumed he'd been involved. Not that it was her business where he was, she reminded herself. Taking one more glance at Abe, she forced herself to get into her car and drive to the shop. If he got into another fight she was confident that Randolph would handle it wisely. She hadn't slept much, thinking about the spray can and what it meant.

It had been nearly nine-thirty when Abe had come into the house, and though he left his boots on the porch, he still smelled like a barn. Mucking that many stalls with only one other person to help was a huge job. Tired, stinky and quiet, he'd disappeared into the hall bathroom. She'd been in her room ordering business supplies for the shop when she'd heard him exit the shower and pad down the hall to his room.

Still feeling conflicted about what to say, she'd given him a few minutes and then knocked lightly on his door. When there was no answer, she'd opened the door. He was already asleep in the dark room. At first, she'd thought he might be pretending in order to avoid talking to her, but there was no faking the soft snores.

Which was a good thing, she'd decided, heading back to her room. Maybe he'd be too tired to get into any more trouble.

Maybe that was another motive behind Randolph's plan.

Too bad some of that sleep hadn't rubbed off on her, she'd thought later as she lay in bed staring up at the ceiling fan. Despite the fact that it had been a long, hectic two days, it seemed she was doomed to let the events roll around in her head with no peace. She'd come here to get help resolving Abe's issues. She hadn't realized when she'd come to Sunrise Ranch that she would also be coming to terms with issues of her own.

Issues she had no idea how to react to.

When she'd finally drifted off to a restless sleep, it was with Tucker's laughing, paint-dotted face squarely in the center of her thoughts.

Tucker gathered the boys up late the evening after picking up the donkeys and ferried them to Chili's ranch to check fence lines. He'd had another crazy day. Though it hadn't involved paint, it had had its own unusual set of odd circumstances—lots of them. A semi driver had fallen asleep and flipped his rig out on the interstate. He'd been carried off to the hospital with minor injuries. Tucker was left to clean up the mess—clean up the chickens, to be exact.

Thousands of squawking chickens! Running, hopping, crazy chickens scattered everywhere—it was bad. He'd had to call all his deputies in to help deal with the traffic and the poultry. The only good thing he had to say about it was that he was wearing a clean, dry uniform.

By the time he and the boys arrived at Chili's place, they were practically rolling on the floorboards laughing at his tale of woe.

They agreed that looking for the donkey escape route was a breeze compared to chasing chickens. Even Abe, though quiet, hadn't been able to hold back a few chuckles. Of course, the kid had been mucking out stalls for two days with twelve more to go. Compared to that, chicken chasing might appeal.

Same with Jake, who seemed fine but stayed clear of Abe. Tucker had brought only the older fellas along, wanting time to observe the two and see if anything came out into the open.

"Welcome, boys," Chili greeted them when they arrived. "Thanks for coming out to look for holes in my fence." He'd driven his truck and trailer out behind Tucker and the boys to the area that ran along the road.

"If we can't find the break, then tomorrow after we work cows, we'll bring the whole crew. The younger boys are wearing their lips on the ground, they were so disappointed that I didn't let them come. I promised them Saturday was their day to ride roughshod on your place if nothing showed up this afternoon."

Chili chuckled. "Them boys are a hoot and a half. Bring 'em on over here. They ain't gonna tear up nothin'."

They got the horses unloaded and everyone saddled up. Though Abe wasn't great on a horse, he was fair. Time in the saddle would improve that naturally.

Chili grunted as he climbed up into the saddle. "I don't saddle up as easy as I used to, with these old creaky bones of mine. But let's ride, boys. If we see something worth looking at it'll be nice to watch all you young 'uns check it out for me.

"I don't recognize you, son," Chili continued, his gaze stalling on Abe. "You must be Suzie's boy. We met her the other day at the shop."

Tucker saw a flash of something volatile in his eyes.

"She's my mom."

"Nice lady. What's your name?"

"Abe." It was more of a grunt.

Tucker didn't like his attitude. "Abe, you're going to ride with me. The others will go with Chili. That way we can split up. That okay with you, Chili?"

"You're the boss," Chili said, shooting Tucker a sharp-eyed look that told him that the older man hadn't missed the bad attitude.

The others had mounted up and within

moments they were riding across Chili's pasture. The boys loved this. They smiled and leaned forward in their saddles. Tucker knew that, if they could, they'd be galloping across the pastures. Instead, he held them back, talking to them about what he wanted them to do when they got there. When they arrived at the fence that ran beside the road, they split up into west or east groups.

"Watch for tracks or anything that alerts you to many donkeys tramping around," he said, as they started out in silence. Abe looked sullen and uninterested.

The sun was out and bright in their eyes. Tucker squinted from beneath his hat at Abe. "So how's it going?" he finally asked.

Abe hiked a shoulder. "It's going."

"You like the boys?"

"Sure. Most of them are okay."

Obviously, Abe was fond of the word *okay.* "You seemed bothered a minute ago. Want to share what that was about?"

He studied the fence intently. "He called me *son*. I didn't like it."

"I thought that might have bothered you."

Abe frowned. "I'm no man's son anymore."

"You will always be Gordon's son."

He shrugged. After a moment he asked, "Did he talk about me much?"

The question shocked Tucker. "He talked about you all the time, Abe. He was proud of you and loved you so much. You and your mother. He showed us pictures all the time. And he said y'all were the best things that ever happened to him."

Abe's Adam's apple bobbed and his nostrils flared, but no tears came. When he looked at Tucker, his eyes were eerily dry. "Do you feel weird being alive and my dad being dead?"

Leave it to kids to cut to the point. "Yes, I do. And I'll never get over feeling like it should have been me and not your dad." Tucker prayed for words that could help this boy. He felt powerless, even more so than he had felt with Suzie. "This may sound stupid and might not be something you want to hear, but God does have a plan. He can make good from bad. Even something this bad."

"Nothing is gonna bring him back. And now I'm riding a fence with you and not my dad."

The blow hit Tucker in the chest. "I'm not going to lie to you. I can apologize till I'm blue in the face and it won't change a thing. But you have a wonderful mom who loves you and a whole support group at the ranch who care for you, me included. And I can promise you that I'll honor your dad by being here for you and your mom till the day I die. I promise you that, even if it doesn't mean much to you now."

Abe stared at him for a long time as the horses moved slowly forward beneath them. This was what riding the range was good for—Tucker and his dad had ridden many a fence line together after his mother's death.

Abe just nodded and went back to studying the fence.

"I'm hoping you'll let go of this anger you're holding in, Abe. It's only going to hurt you," Tucker added.

With the fighting incident, it was time to do something. He needed Abe to be comfortable with him, so he could build a bridge of trust.

"So?"

Tucker hated his sullenness. Sometimes hurt seemed all there was. "Well, I'm here if you need me. And I'm here to keep you out of trouble, too, standing in for your dad, so remember that."

His shoulders stiff, Abe rode ahead, leaving Tucker a few yards behind. It was going to be another long afternoon. But this was a complicated puzzle of the heart—a child's heart—and Tucker planned to tread very carefully.

* * *

Two weeks after she'd arrived in town, Suzie opened her shop. It was both nerve-racking and exciting at the same time. To her surprise, everyone came to wish her well, creating a grand opening that she would never forget.

She had planned on getting opened and then, after settling in and getting some orders under her belt, she would have an open house or something, but on the Saturday morning she was actually going to start business, in walked Mabel, Ms. Jo and Nana with trays of refreshments and decorations.

"Good morning!" Mabel exclaimed, first in the door. "We are here to party! And help out any way we can."

"Oh, what? Why?" Suzie stumbled over her words as they marched through the door and took over.

"You just go about your business," Ms. Jo said. "We've got this under control."

"That's right," Nana said. "By eleven, this place will be a regular Grand Central station."

Flustered and touched, Suzie hugged each of them and went back to arranging her very first preordered flower arrangement. Chili had looked a little green around the collar when she'd asked him if he still wanted it, and she'd thought he was going to back out. Then Drewbaker had grinned as if knowing he'd planned to back out all along, and Chili had staunchly reiterated that he did, indeed, want the order.

So here she was working on a bouquet of sunflowers. She had to admit she was curious about who they were for. When she'd asked Chili what he wanted in the bouquet he'd been specific: sunflowers and magenta zinnias. As she was putting the arrangement together, she couldn't help but wonder if Chili had any idea what the meaning of these flowers were.

Surely not. He was an old rancher who

barely set foot in a florist's and had admitted such. True, the colors complemented each other, but then, any deep rose-colored flower could have done the same.

Sunflowers and magenta zinnias: adoration and lasting affection.

Who, Suzie wanted to know, did Chili adore with lasting affection?

"That is beautiful," Nana said, coming to stand beside her. "I adore sunflowers, don't you?"

"Very much so." Suzie's radar went up—could it be? "Nana, can I ask about your husband?"

Nana got a gentle look in her eye. "I'm seventy-two and he's been gone nearly thirty years now, but not a day goes by that I don't think of Harrison Randolph McDermott. When you've been loved by and loved a man like my Harry, you never forget. Oops, I left the plates in the truck. I better run and get them."

Suzie watched her go. She didn't know

what had happened to Nana's Harry, but Nana had been somewhere near fifty when he'd died. And she was strong, independent, and had done amazing things with this ranch and these boys.

She inspired Suzie to require more of herself than she had, so far. A person had to move past grief. Past anger.

A person had to move forward.

Taking in her shop with the colorful gift items and the silk arrangements and colorful vases, she felt a flicker of joy ignite inside of her.

She smiled.

If she could feel this, surely Abe would feel it someday soon.

There was movement outside the window as cars and trucks began pulling into the parking spaces. Within moments, the grand opening was in full swing.

Tucker came in, right behind Chili and Drewbaker. And by that time, there was hardly room to move around in the small front space. "Congratulations," he said, over the laughter and hum of conversation. "It looks great in here, and I assume there isn't any evidence in the back room of any heinous crimes being committed."

She laughed. "No, there isn't. All the evidence of the terrible crime I committed has been destroyed. How is your shirt?"

"I'm afraid it didn't survive."

"I was afraid of that." She sighed. "But I'd be glad to replace it."

"Thanks, but no need for that. I have a closetful. Those are pretty," he said, nodding toward the arrangement.

"Yes. My first order."

"Are those the ones from Chili?"

"Yes, and I have to say the man knows his flowers. I'm very curious."

Tucker's smile spread wide and his eyes crinkled around the edges.

"You know who they're for, don't you? No, don't tell me. I'll wait until he tells me." Was her suspicion right? Were they for Nana?

"I wasn't going to say anything. But yes, I'm fairly certain I know who they're for. It should be interesting."

"That's what Drewbaker said the day Chili ordered them."

He laughed. "Only because it's true," he said, just as she saw Drewbaker spot the flowers from across the room.

She knew he had, because he elbowed Chili in the ribs and pointed straight at them.

Chili turned, and his head ducked momentarily, as if looking for a table to crawl under.

"Those must be your flowers, Chili," Drewbaker roared.

Chili gulped, his Adam's apple bobbing low. "Maybe so," he said, glancing around.

Beside Suzie, Tucker chuckled softly. "Like I said, interesting."

Edwina, Ms. Jo's waitress, had popped in

for the party and her gritty voice rose over the crowd. "Well, Chili, you old Romeo, those are beautiful—not that I've ever gotten flowers. My four ex-husbands' idea of giving me flowers was to buy me a roll of flower-printed paper towels. Don't laugh," she said, dryly. "I kid you not."

From across the room, Suzie saw Nana spin, her thick gray ponytail swinging out like a horse's mane. Her gaze hit Chili and the little man turned redder than Tucker's shirt had been during the paint fiasco.

And in that instant, Suzie knew she'd been right. She glanced at Tucker.

"Yup. Head over heels for her for years. Poor fella."

"I had no idea until moments ago. Would never have dreamed it. They, well, they just don't fit."

"The heart doesn't always listen to reality," Tucker said, holding her gaze for a beat too long. Suzie's knees melted momentarily as her heart bucked. "You're in the flower business. I'd think you'd know that."

While they'd been speaking, Chili pushed his chest forward and marched across the room to her. "You did a fine job on those. May I take them?"

"S-sure," she said, hurrying around the counter and handing the flowers over. "Do you want a card?"

There was startling determination in his eyes. "Nope. No card needed. Ruby Ann McDermott knows everything there is about a flower. She'll read the message in the flowers themselves."

Suzie's heart skipped a beat. His message: I adore you with lasting affection.

He crossed the room straight to Nana. "Ruby Ann, if anyone deserves flowers, it'd be you."

Shocked though she was, Nana took the beautiful green vase in her arms and studied the flowers. "They're lovely. And I thank you," she said. Beside her, Ms. Jo and Mabel were actually speechless.

Chili thrust his chest out a little more, and beamed. "You're welcome." That said, he strode—no, he strutted to the door.

"Now, don't go getting ideas," Nana called after him, and Suzie thought she saw alarm in Nana's usually calm eyes.

Was Chili listening? No. He just grinned and continued out the door. It really was a great exit.

"I have to give him credit. He cowboy'd up on that one," Tucker said. "Nana needed that."

"Really?"

He looked at her. "Every woman needs flowers. Even if she thinks she doesn't. I've got to go to work."

Her pulse skipped at his low declaration. He turned to go.

"Tucker, wait. How did Abe act when you took them to ride fence at Chili's?" She'd meant to ask him earlier.

"It was all right. He's wound up tight, like you said. I talked to him a little. He asked about Gordon. The good thing was, he did talk some. And he asked a few questions. I take that as a good thing. But he's expressing his feelings with action. So keep an eye out, and call me anytime, day or night, if you're worried about anything. You might try to set him up with a counselor. Whether he wants it or not. I think he might need it."

"Thanks," she said.

His radio crackled to life. "Duty calls," he said, and tipped his hat.

This had been a great day, but she would give it all up to have Abe happy again.

This girl didn't want flowers, she just wanted her son happy. And she didn't want to have to call for help—she'd much rather not need it.

Chapter Eight

She didn't have to call Tucker; he called her later that day, right after lunch. He asked what time she was closing, and when she told him two o'clock, he asked her if she wanted to go with him and all the boys to check fences at Chili's.

She said no, at first, until he reminded her it would be good to spend time doing something with Abe. Of course she agreed to that.

Now she was riding shotgun beside Tucker in his truck full of boys as he led the other trucks across the pastures toward a stand of trees.

It looked as if it was snowing in the middle of May.

"I thought you'd like to see this," he said, pulling to a halt.

Suzie stepped out of Tucker's truck and stared at the huge trees that he'd parked beneath. Cottonwoods.

"I've never seen this many of them together!" It was a beautiful sight when the cotton tufts floated from the branches in a slow free fall to earth.

She'd seen one or two in yards, but there had to be fifteen in this shady cluster. "These trees are amazing! And huge," she said, opening her arms and turning in the midst of the falling cotton.

"What is this stuff?" B.J., the youngest boy, asked. He immediately began jumping and diving, trying to catch handfuls of the downy fluff. "It looks like snow."

All the younger boys joined him in running after the floaters. The older boys, Abe included, were helping unload the trailers of horses.

"I've always liked this spot, this time of year," Tucker said, coming to stand beside her. Smiling down at her, he plucked a bit of cotton from her hair. "It looks good on you," he said, holding the small piece of fuzz up for her to see.

She wasn't thinking about the cotton any longer. "Which way will we go?" she asked, butterflies shifting in her chest.

"Which way do you want to go?"

She stared at him, her insides completely aflutter. "I…" She looked to the left, then to the right and back at him. "I don't know." Were they talking about which way to go to check fences? His deep blue eyes were steady and unwavering as they seemed to see every emotional hiding place within her.

Which way did she want to go?

Looking at Tucker she was suddenly filled with the longing to be free to feel again.

She wished, at least for a little while,

to be free from the bitterness and the grief that bound her.

Tucker couldn't tear his gaze away from Suzie in the soft white rain from the huge old cottonwood trees. She was beautiful. He'd enjoyed talking and laughing with her at the grand opening that morning…. Now he wanted to pull her into his arms and kiss her beneath the cottonwoods.

Wanted to be more to her than the man she held responsible for making her a widow.

He wanted to kiss her and wipe all of her fears and worries and sadness away.

"I better get the horses so we can ride the fence." Spinning away, he strode toward the older boys. Abe and Jake were leading horses out of the trailer, and Caleb and Tony were busy unloading the other horses from the trailer Tony had driven over. He'd gotten his license the day before and was one proud kid.

Tucker waved the four over. "Y'all know

what to do. I'm sending you east along the line and I'll take the younger ones in the opposite direction. Tony, you have the cell. Call me if y'all find anything. I know you'll do a great job. Abe, I'd like you to come with us—"

"I'd like to go with the guys," he said, his expression tight.

Tucker studied him, then Jake. "You two going to get along? No fighting—and I mean none."

Jake nodded. "Fine by me."

"Me, too." Abe rubbed the back of his neck and let out a hard breath.

"Do I have your word?"

Both teens nodded.

"Fine, I'm going to trust that you'll do this job, and I'm going to hope that you have a good time. I still don't know what's going on between the two of you, but here's another chance to prove you're mending your differences. You both did good work with the stalls."

"Yes, sir," Jake said readily, making Tucker more and more certain that whatever had happened between the two had more to do with Abe than Jake.

"Yes, sir," Abe said a moment later.

"Good. See you in three hours."

Seconds later they rode off. He'd watched many men head out under his command, and it felt good to know these boys weren't riding out into a war zone.

"I thought I was supposed to be spending time with Abe," Suzie said, coming up beside him.

"Yeah, about that. Abe wanted to ride with the older guys."

"He and Jake okay?"

"I think so. They promised they wouldn't fight."

She smiled. "Then that's a very good thing."

"Even if you're stuck with me and the rowdy bunch?"

She winced. "I'll manage." She chuckled,

looking toward the boys playing in the summer snowstorm. "We better head out, or they'll be trying to ski soon."

"True. Thanks for coming," he said, then called the boys to mount up. They shot up from wrestling in the cotton. It was stuck to them like chicken feathers as they raced each other to their horses.

"This will be fun," Suzie said, taking him by surprise. "Thank you for inviting me. I haven't ridden that much in my life." She stared critically at the horse he'd untied for her.

"This is our trusty Cupcake. She'll do right by you."

"I learned on ol' Cupcake and she's a good ol' horse," Sammy called. "She won't toss you."

"She sure won't," B.J. agreed. "I learned on her, too."

The other boys all joined in encouraging her as they nudged closer on their horses to encircle them.

Suzie laughed. "Thanks, boys, I need your support."

Grabbing the saddle horn, she stuck her foot into the stirrup and hauled herself up, then threw her leg over. Cupcake stood docile as a kitten, making Tucker proud of the old horse.

"There you go," he said, moving to stand at her knee and handing her the reins. "You'll be fine." He snagged his own horse's reins and stepped up and into the saddle. "Okay, let's head out. You boys can lead the way. Here we go." Tucker went ahead of Suzie and knew that Cupcake would follow. It wouldn't take a lot of experience or work on Suzie's part today. "Just give her a nudge when she slows down too much, or a little pressure with your knees, and that should do it."

He held his horse at a slow walk while she got adjusted to Cupcake. "See, you're doing good."

"Thanks," she said. "And thanks for helping with Abe."

"We'll just keep letting him be more and more a part of the family."

"So, how did the party go after I left?" he asked, enjoying her riding beside him more than he should.

"You saw the highlight. The rest was just friendly chitchat. Much of it was about Nana's flowers. I'll confess, the shop makes me a little nervous."

"Really, what part?"

She hesitated. "Not the actual designing. But the actual running of the business." She took a deep breath and expelled it slowly. "I never finished school. I dropped out right before my senior year."

"Really? What happened that caused you to drop out of school? That doesn't fit." He was shocked she'd done such a thing and knew there had to be a reason.

"It was just my mom and me. And Mom got really ill. She was in and out of the hospital and we needed the money, so I went to work full time as a waitress."

"I'm sorry." Her doing that fit with the kind of person he'd come to know her as. "How's your mom?"

"She passed away at the end of that year. I met Gordon not long after she died and we got married. I could have gone back to school, but I got pregnant."

"So you didn't go back."

"No."

"That happens a lot. So, now, trying to open your own business makes you nervous."

"It does. But I'll make it. I just feel like I'm faking it or something. Does that sound odd?"

He studied the fence and glanced at the boys ahead to make sure they weren't getting too wild. "Have you ever thought about going back to school? Maybe get your GED and then some college courses. It would eliminate that fake sense that you have, and it would also be a positive move for you with Abe. It's always good for kids to see their parents work for a goal and accomplish it."

She grew quiet and stared ahead, deep in thought. "I honestly have toyed with that idea, especially since Gordon's death."

"You know," he added, "Jolie is a good person to ask about that, I'm sure."

"I'm sure she would be a help." Suzie smiled. "I think I'll talk to her. And find a place to take the course." Reaching across the distance between them she touched his arm. "Thank you."

Her touch was warm, and Tucker wanted to place his hand over hers and hold tight. "No thanks necessary," he said, his voice tight with wanting things he could never have.

"Suzie," he said, gently. "Gordon would be proud of what you're doing. You should know that. Everything you're doing is for Abe's welfare."

She raked her fingers through her hair. "I hope so. I was so very proud of him."

"We found it!"

The whoop and excited yells came from the boys.

"I better go see what they've found." Tucker urged his horse into a trot and headed toward the boys, though his thoughts were not on finding the donkey escape route anymore. He was thinking how his skin still radiated with the touch of Suzie's hand. And wondering what it would be like for Suzie to be proud of him.

To have that soft edge to her eyes when she thought of him, the way she did when she thought of Gordon.

It was wrong to even think about wanting that.

But he did.

He was in so much trouble.

The remodeled barn that housed Lucy's paint studio was full of silk flowers, lace and ribbons. They'd been having a great Girls' Night, as they were calling it, while they worked on decorations for Lucy's upcoming wedding. Suzie had enjoyed the first Monday of business at her flower shop. There'd been a lot of traffic. She'd sold several gift and home decor items, and filled a few orders for flowers. It had been a very encouraging day.

And now she was enjoying helping with Lucy's decorations. Lucy had tried to pay her for her services but she'd refused. They'd finally come to an agreement that she would do the flowers for the wedding party and her bouquet for a price. Lucy had been adamant about that and so Suzie had agreed. After all, as Lucy had pointed out, she was running a business and had to show a profit. Suzie knew she was right.

Still, looking at the room, satisfaction and joy filled her to be pitching in as a friend on this part of the decorating. It was her way of paying back some of the goodness they'd shown her and Abe.

And it was beautiful. Greenery wrapped around wreaths with small daisies scattered throughout them were garnished with ribbons in silky cream and soft fern colors. To add sparkle and romance, the women were also decorating twig balls with tiny lights and ribbons. These would hang suspended throughout the reception hall.

Suzie and Jolie were working together to attach tiny strings of lights to large twig balls.

Suzie decided now was a good time to ask for help. Being a private person, opening up about her past was hard, especially to someone as accomplished as Jolie. But she trusted her new friend.

"Jolie, I never finished high school and I've been thinking I'd like to get my GED. Can you help me with that?"

Jolie's eyes lit up like fireflies. "I would love to help you! It's wonderful you've decided to do this. So many people never finish for a wide array of reasons. Trying again will be a good example for Abe."

"That's the major determining factor. Tucker, actually, is the one who pushed me to do it. We were talking, and I told him I hadn't finished school. And that I felt a little intimidated, opening my own business. He suggested I might feel better if I had that certificate. And I might go on to do some community college courses."

"I think that's a great idea. I'll check into it first thing tomorrow. What grade level were you at?"

Suzie said she just lacked twelfth grade when she'd had to quit. "I don't regret what I did. I'm glad I was able to help out with my mom being so ill. I don't know what would have happened if I hadn't." With no other family, it struck her again how important it was to have Abe here, at the ranch.

"Raising a child on my own is no easy task and there is that fear that if something happened to me, if I were to get ill, like my mother did, what would happen to Abe? I'm glad he has you and everyone here at the ranch to count as family."

Jolie leaned across the table and grabbed her hand. "We're so glad y'all are here."

They worked and talked about what getting the GED would consist of. After a while Jolie asked, "Do you ever think of remarrying?"

The question took Suzie by surprise. "I haven't." Tucker flashed before her and her insides tilted uneasily. "I'm not sure I can risk it, for one. It's scary thinking about falling in love and running the risk of losing him again."

If she ever did feel she was ready to take that risk, it would be with someone who had a desk job.

Not a military man. Not a lawman.

"You know, from what I've heard about Gordon, he would want you to be happy."

Suzie tugged the ribbon a little harder

than needed at the top of the ball she was working on. "I'm doing all right."

"Sure you are. You're doing great. But Gordon sounds like a guy who would want you to move on, to find someone else to be a part of your life, yours and Abe's."

"You're right, that's what he would have wanted. But this is about what I want now." Suzie studied the finished ball, lost in memories for a moment. "I met Gordon right after my mother died. He was stationed in San Antonio working in the recruitment office. I fell for him instantly. And you're right, he was a giving guy. We only dated two months before we got married."

"Really, that sounds like Lucy and Rowdy."

Suzie smiled at that. "Some people think that's crazy. But it isn't."

She'd never been instantly attracted to anyone the way she'd been attracted to Gordon. Never.

That's a lie, and you know it. The words whispered through her mind and caused her heart to ache. *You felt similar attraction that first day when Tucker wrapped his arm around your shoulders and you looked into his eyes.*

She pushed the thoughts from her head. Things were so tangled. *This is the man you hold responsible for Gordon's death.*

Didn't she? He'd been so good to them. He held himself responsible. But even if she no longer held Tucker responsible for Gordon's death, he would never be someone she could consider marrying. Those emotions were still too tangled up. Besides, he might be a sheriff in a small town, but he still put his life on the line every day. Death was still a possibility every time he strapped on his gun and pinned on his badge.

Why was she even entertaining these thoughts about Tucker?

They were on a tenuous tightrope toward friendship, and for the sake of their common goal—Abe's health and happiness—friendship made sense.

Anything else did not.

That she felt irresistibly drawn to him in moments when her guard was down didn't matter. That was understandable.

Admitting that those emotions were there eased the tight knot of tension in her chest just a little. It was…explainable.

She'd been young and vulnerable when she'd met and fallen for Gordon. She was not so young anymore, but she was vulnerable again. Gordon had helped her during the loss of her mother. Tucker was helping her with Abe, with coping with the aftermath of Gordon's death. Completely explainable.

She had no one else to turn to and Tucker, along with his family, was filling that void.

Yes, having her shop open and finishing her education would help fix that. Knowledge equaled strength and stability for her.

Exactly what she needed.

Chapter Nine

Tucker was running late as he turned his SUV onto the blacktop road and headed toward the ranch. Everyone would understand, though; his job had a timetable all its own. This time he'd been called out to aid in a domestic violence case in a neighboring small town. No matter how many times he did it, he would never get used to responding to a case and finding a female with a bruised and bloody face. But there had been a twist to the scenario: the male, after having beaten his wife, had been the one to call 911 when she'd retaliated with a baseball bat.

Tucker had arrived on the scene first to find the man had actually climbed a tree to get away from his fed up, abused wife.

Tucker took one look at her face and the man had been ordered from the tree, handcuffed and escorted to jail. Tucker hoped she would press charges. But he had learned that most times people didn't. Still, today, he had hope. Thinking about the lowlife cowering in the tree had him chuckling as he drove toward the ranch.

It had taken a long time after losing Gordon for Tucker to smile again. He'd been different when he'd finally come home after spending time in the hospital. Making the stop to see Suzie and offer his condolences, and his aid and support, hadn't helped him. She'd been so angry—so grief-stricken and full of blame toward him that it had cut him to the bone. Helping Gordon's family had been his only means of redemption and when Suzie refused him, it crushed that option.

He'd been in a very dark hole.

It had taken his family a long time to talk him into running for sheriff. But in the end, God had led him to accept the post. Most days, small-town sheriff duties were about as redneck as could be, what with chasing chickens and herding escaped donkeys. But then, times like today, when he got to see the human spirit fight back against wrong, and he got the opportunity to be a part of that—he knew he was making a difference. And that was his redemption.

Now that Abe and Suzie were here, he'd come full circle. God was giving him the opportunity to make a difference in the life of Gordon's family.

If he just didn't mess it up.

And that meant he had to stop thinking about Suzie standing in the sunlight, cotton in her hair, and eyes as sparkling and changing as the ocean.

Eyes he continually found himself getting lost in.

No, he needed to focus on the life he'd been dealt, the good he was able to do and the wrongs his job enabled him to right.

With Suzie, he had been careful. And he would be, not because of his own feelings, but because his getting in too deep would harm the friendship and trust that he needed to build with Suzie.

Anything more, any romantic notions that continually knocked the wind out of him when he looked into her eyes, were absolutely off-limits.

Rolling to a halt in front of the horse barn, he rammed the shifter into Park with more power than needed, just to ram home the thoughts in his head.

He was here to see Wes and Joseph. They were arriving home from college today to attend Rowdy and Lucy's wedding in two days. Tucker had to be at the ranch to welcome them home.

"Hey, Dad. Pepper," he said, walking over t o the stable, where his dad stood with Walter Pepper, their horse foreman. "Have you heard from them? Are they running on time?"

Nana had had someone string a welcome-home banner across the front of the chow hall and folks were arriving for the welcome party they were throwing Wes and Joseph.

Pepper's sky-blue eyes crinkled at the edges, standing out against his pure white hair. "I'd say those two might not make it till tomorrow, but then they haven't had Nana's cooking in three months, so I'm sure they have the pedal to the metal and will be here by two o'clock, just like they said."

Randolph hiked a black brow, reminding Tucker of George Strait with his black hair, lean face and easygoing smile. "I agree with Pepper. Haven't heard from them, but I'm sure they'll be here on time. If not, their nana will probably jump in her truck and go looking for them. Or expect you to turn on the missing-persons alert sirens."

"True." Tucker looked at his watch. "Well, they have ten minutes." Suzie was standing beside Nana. She wore a soft turquoise blouse with her jeans and was as fresh as a flower. He couldn't look away—and just like that, she caught him staring. The small, tight smile she sent him was enough to cause his pulse to break the speed limit. He smiled in reaction then forced himself to turn back to the conversation.

"There they come!" A shout went up from the boys in the arena as a black truck sped over the hill, dust flying out behind it. Sixteen boys scrambled from every corner of the yard, arena and horse barn. They came running with whoops and yells and laughter.

His dad crossed his arms and smiled in satisfaction. "Tucker, your mother would be proud. That right there…" He nodded toward the gathering of excited boys as Wes and Joseph came to a halt. Wes had his cowboy hat hanging out the window and was waving and yelling, while Joseph drove and waved and grinned. "That right there is family. Just like Lydia wanted it to be."

Tucker's throat tightened. His mother had had a dream. And it had come true over and over again across the years at Sunrise Ranch. And it gave him purpose and meaning, knowing that he'd had a part in it and would continue to have a part in it as long as he was breathing.

Looking across the way at Abe, and then at Suzie, he knew they were witnessing how it had been for Gordon. And he hoped Abe's heart was more and more at peace being here.

Suzie watched, amazed at the excitement of the boys as their friends jumped from the truck. One was a stout, happy-faced young man with blond curls and eyes full of mischief. The other was tall and lanky with a long, thin face and the kindest brown eyes she'd ever seen.

The happy-faced one grinned, opened his arms wide and yelled, "Hey, hey, little brothers. What's up?"

The younger boys literally tackled him, yelling, "Wes, Wes!"

The pure tenderness of the show of affection between them was beautiful.

"Glad y'all are home, Joseph," Tony said, hugging the kind-eyed young man.

He laughed. "It's good to be here. Wes always steals the show, though," he teased.

"Hey, we can jump on you, too, but we're a little big for that," Jake offered, and hugged him followed by Caleb. Joseph didn't have to wait long before the younger ones finished mugging Wes and came after him with just as much excitement. They'd been gone and now they were home.

It hit her in that moment that these weren't friends. These truly were brothers in all the best senses of the word. There was a camaraderie they shared that was touching. And she marveled more at what the McDermotts had accomplished.

Gordon had told her that they'd changed his life. The day the social worker pulled his file and decided that he, a teenager who'd been abandoned by his parents as a toddler then bounced from one foster home to the next, was a perfect fit for the new boys ranch that had just opened up. He'd told her that, but until this moment it hadn't hit her how deeply he'd meant what he'd said.

"Okay, okay," Nana called, moving into the fray. "Now it's my turn. Come give your nana some lovin' hugs, boys."

Instantly Wes broke free and grabbed Nana in a bear hug. Then Joseph did the same. Nana laughed and teared up—so did Suzie as she watched.

After Nana had her hugs, the McDermott men moved in and there was a bunch of manly handshaking and more bear hugs. It was clear that Tucker and his dad and brothers had true love and affection for Wes and Joseph.

"Hubba-hubba," Wes said, when Jolie stepped up and gave him a hug. Looking over Jolie's shoulder, he winked at Morgan. "I'm still in love."

Jolie chuckled, grabbed his beat-up hat off his head and scrubbed his curls. "It's good to have you home, funny man. Joseph, give me a hug." Reaching over, she engulfed him. "It's good to have you both home."

Then it was Lucy's turn, and it was the same warm welcome.

Abe stood to the side and took it all in.

"Hey, dude," Wes said, moving his way. "You're new. What's your name?"

"Abe."

Wes's brows lifted and his eyes twinkled like Christmas lights. "Well, Abe, my man, you're going to have to hang with me and Joseph some before we head back to school. Got to get to know our new brother."

Abe shrugged. "Sure."

Wes reaching out to Abe had Suzie's eyes misting up again, even though Abe wasn't as receptive as she'd hoped he would be. These boys had learned to be inclusive living here on the ranch. It came naturally to them. Suzie stepped out of the way toward the chow hall, not wanting to mar the moment with tears. This was how Gordon had grown up. She could only imagine the welcome he would have had if he'd have come home from war.

"Are you all right?" Tucker asked, coming up behind her. She hadn't even realized he was near.

She hadn't seen him since she'd checked fences with him and the boys almost a week ago. It seemed longer than that. "I'm fine. Just overwhelmed by the reunion. Gordon truly did have a home here, didn't he?"

"Yes. And Gordon was, in many ways, like Wes there. He was a warm kid with a willingness to take care of others, and he did it by teasing the dickens out of them most of the time. Little kids loved Gordon."

"That sounds like him. I'm sure he was like that with the guys in his unit, too."

Tucker held her eyes, steady and sure. "Yes, he was. He led by example."

Led by example.

The phrase drove deep into her heart. That was what heroes did, and he'd led by example right to his death. She pushed the thoughts away. Gordon was a hero in every sense of the word. It was just hard to accept that it had cost them all so much.

"I guess Rowdy is as excited about the wedding as Lucy is."

"He was ready the day he asked her five months ago."

"It will be a lovely wedding."

Tucker smiled. She knew he knew that she was diverting the conversation away from Gordon.

"I'm excited for them," he said. "It's been great watching how the Lord has worked in both Morgan's and Rowdy's lives. I've always wanted the best for my brothers and they're getting that in Jolie and Lucy."

That suddenly had Suzie wondering about him. "Have you ever been in love, Tucker?" Why was she asking him this? *Because you need to know.*

Was that sadness or anger she saw flash in the depths of his deep, deep blue eyes?

"Not me," he said. "I've never been marriage material. Hey, I need to get back. Do you want to walk over and let me introduce you while I give 'em a hug before I head back to work?"

"Sure," she said, following him as he'd started walking without waiting for her answer. Wes and Joseph hugged him, grinning so wide their faces had to hurt. They were well loved.

"This is Suzie, Abe's mother. Abe's dad, Gordon, was part of our family here, too, when he was younger." Tucker introduced her as soon as the hugging stopped. Then she was swept into conversation with the young men, and Nana joined in on the conversation, too. Tucker took his leave and headed to his truck.

Suzie's gaze followed him as he climbed into his SUV, which stirred up dust as he left. She wondered if it would be another week before she saw him again, and then remembered absently that he would be at the wedding in two days.

Funny, how that suddenly seemed a long time away.

It wasn't until a few minutes later, when she was helping serve the feast that Nana had made, that Suzie realized Abe hadn't come to load up a plate of food like the other teens. Looking around, she spotted him riding a horse alone at the far end of the large arena.

She watched him for a few minutes. *Please, Lord,* she found herself praying... *Please.*

She didn't even put words to the pleading prayer. God knew what she was asking. God knew what Abe needed.

As if God knew what *she* needed, Nana came up beside her and watched Abe ride, too. "He'll come around, you know. I've seen boys work out their grief, their abandonment, any number of issues of the heart and soul."

Suzie sighed. "It would be wonderful if he was just a regular kid out there riding for the love of riding."

"One day he will be. You just keep thinking about that. Every day is one day closer to that day."

Suzie had hired Camy, a high school student, to work a few hours in the afternoons, and today was her first day. It had worked out well, giving Suzie the time to help with the welcome-home party for Wes and Joseph. It was after five, and Suzie was feeling restless as she headed back to town to make sure Camy had locked up good. She also wanted to begin Lucy's wedding bouquet while it was quiet and no one was popping in and out. She'd been touched when Lucy had decided to forgo simple silk arrangements and hired Suzie to do the wedding party flowers.

When Suzie told Abe she was going to be in town for the evening, he'd surprised her by wanting to go, too.

Any hope she'd had that he might be a happy companion was immediately dashed when he got into the car, slammed the door and sulked in the passenger seat.

Anger flashed through Suzie, her patience wearing thin. "Abe, what is wrong with you? It was a nice afternoon. Didn't you like Wes and Joseph?"

"Yeah, sure, Mom. It was one big happy family out there. It always is. Only I don't want that family. I want my dad."

"Of course you do."

He was at an age when he really needed his dad.

"I want to go home. Back to San Antonio."

"Our home is here now, Abe. All you did there was get into trouble. It's better here. You'll fit in better every day."

Even though she was watching the road intently, her hands gripping the steering wheel as if it were her last great hope, she could feel his angry glare.

"They're too happy, Mom!"

"Too happy?" She shot him a glance, disbelieving that he was serious. He was, though, his dark expression made that clear.

"It's like they all just got to the ranch and suddenly everything was wonderful."

She pulled into her parking space in front of the shop. "I don't understand, Abe. I don't."

His voice had been rising with each declaration. "Their lives were crummy before they got here. Lousy. Their dads were deadbeats, drunks and losers. Their home lives were the pits. Jake's was so bad he was on the street! And he was trying to tell me everything was going to be A-okay. I told him he was only saying that because he didn't know any better. I knew better. My dad was great, Mom. You were great."

His voice dropped low. "We were happy. I *know* what I lost. Don't you get it?"

Suzie did. Looking at him she finally understood what he was feeling, what he was struggling with. Tears blinded her as she reached out to touch him.

He yanked away. "I want to go home," he snapped. He jerked on the door handle then thrust open the door. Before Suzie could find her voice he had flung himself from the car and charged across the street. He disappeared within seconds.

Chapter Ten

"This way." Tucker directed the dangerously inebriated man through the side door of the jailhouse. Handcuffed as he was, the man was in danger of stumbling and sprawling onto the concrete floor with no way to break his fall. Tucker had a firm grip on the foul-smelling, somewhat subdued man, not wanting to have to spend the rest of what had turned out to be a miserable day in the emergency room because of this yahoo.

"Whoa," Cody said, swinging his boots off the desk where he'd had them crossed while reclining in his seat. "I can smell him from here."

Tucker frowned. "Well, it's about to get worse. He's all yours. Watch out for his right hook."

The drunk ran off a string of slurred words that Tucker didn't even try to decipher. He was just glad he'd pulled him over when he did, or someone might have been hurt or killed.

"Thanks for the heads-up. Okay, that is just wrong," Cody said, leaning back as he got a whiff up close.

Tucker headed straight for the sink by the coffeepot in the corner and washed his hands.

The door of the office opened, and he turned to see Suzie, pale and teary-eyed, rush inside.

"Suzie, what's going on?"

"It's Abe. He's run off."

"At the ranch?"

She shook her head, swiping her eyes with her fingertips. "Just now."

He grabbed a tissue from the box on the

sidebar and handed it to her. "Here? Tell me what's happened."

"Just a few minutes ago. He ran off. He wanted to ride into town with me and was upset. Tucker, part of what happened between him and Jake was he said some terrible things to Jake about how bad his life had been, and that Jake didn't understand how good Abe's had been. He doesn't want to fit in here. He wants his old life back—his life with me and Gordon in San Antonio."

Poor kid. And Suzie, Tucker had to fight not to pull her close and wipe her tears away. "Let's go find him," he said. He took a second to stick his head through the door to the back of the jail and tell Cory he was going out. "He can't have gone far," he said, reassuring Suzie as he took her arm and led her onto the deserted street. Dew Drop wasn't the busiest place after stores closed down at five. People were in and out of the Spotted Cow Café, but the stores on the square were pretty much shut down.

Suzie had stopped crying now; he was glad. He wasn't real comfortable with tears. Growing up with all guys and then joining the marines didn't give him a lot of experience with tears. And Suzie's tears cut straight to his heart.

"Thanks for helping me. He ran across the street, toward the inn, but I didn't see which street he went down."

Tucker's office was on a side street just off the square. "We'd better take the SUV. We can make better time than on foot." He led her around the corner of the building to where his vehicle was parked. Within moments they were driving across town.

"Let's go down the alley beside the Dew Drop Inn first and then we'll start the backstreets. He'll turn up." He gave her a reassuring smile. "Our streets are about as safe as you can get. So that's a positive."

"That's what I keep telling myself. I know he's safe. He's just so upset."

Tucker was scanning the backs of the

buildings as he drove down the road that cut behind the buildings on that side of town. Suzie was doing the same.

"Tucker, I have to find a way to help Abe be stronger. I don't want this to make him grow up feeling sorry for himself. Which is what I think is happening. Does that make sense? Or does that sound terrible on my part? It's been two years. And I'm afraid I may have contributed to this without realizing it."

"It makes sense. You want him to be a survivor and take control, not let the loss of his dad be something that ruins his life. I'm not sure what you mean about your contributing to it, though."

She looked at him. "He knows how I've held this grudge against you. He's seen the anger in me. The problem I've had blaming you for Gordon's death. I'm sorry about that, Tucker. I've realized I was wrong."

He'd stopped at a stop sign and stared

straight ahead as he took in her words. "You don't have anything to be sorry about."

She reached across the space between them, placing her hand on his forearm. "No—I do. Gordon was a U.S. marine. A *marine*. You know more than anyone what that means. You know what that commitment is. Gordon was a hero. He made choices that were true to the man he was. I accept that. I should have done that before now. I let my anger and…some self-pitying attitude overpower my thoughts."

What did he say to that? She didn't give him a chance to figure it out as she continued.

"You were the one that pointed out that Gordon led by example. And you're right. He did." She smiled. "I've spent two years stealing that from him. His son should have been taught to be proud of what his dad did. But no, I overshadowed his bravery and his sacrifice by putting blame on you. I've led by example, and it was a bad example."

Tucker's heart was thundering in his chest from the touch of her hands and the sincerity in her eyes. Her words didn't take away the guilt he felt toward himself for being alive while Gordon was dead. But it made him proud of Suzie. "That means a great deal to me. Gordon deserves that respect. It's going to be all right. Abe's stronger than he thinks."

"Yes, he is."

Tucker drove across the street and began scanning the area again. The elementary school was on this side of town. On a hunch Tucker hung a left and drove toward the back of the school. And there was Abe. He had climbed to the top of the nine-foot slide and was sitting with his feet on the ladder. He looked about as alone as a kid could be.

"There he is." He pointed, drawing Suzie's gaze from where she'd been scanning the houses across the road.

"Praise the Lord," she said, softly.

Tucker pulled into the empty parking space on the street and they walked across the playground. Abe watched them. The sun was starting to lower in the sky. Purple and blue streaks glowed behind Abe on the slide.

Tucker started praying as they walked. Suzie was right. Abe was going to have to get stronger. Something bad had happened in his life. He'd lost a parent and it was a wrong and terrible thing to happen to a kid. Tucker knew from experience. But he and his brothers had each gone through their own mourning period and then they'd moved on. They'd grown from it and used it to become the adults they knew would have pleased their mother. But they'd each had a rough go of it.

Abe would have to find that within himself, and the truth was that only Abe could do it. Abe would have to make the choice of how he would let, not only his father's death, but his life and sacrifice, affect him. Just as Tucker and Suzie were having to do.

Life went on. No matter what, the wheels of life stopped for no one. Tucker prayed for strength for Abe. And peace.

He prayed for the same for Suzie.

But for himself—until Suzie and Abe were okay, there would be no peace.

Abe looked sullen and Suzie could tell by the redness around his eyes that he'd been crying. Her mind was whirling—what did she need to say to him?

Instead of glaring at her he stared down at her with zero emotion. His face was lax and his eyes dull as if he'd been so furious moments ago that he'd exhausted everything he had.

"Abe, are you okay?" No, it was clear to see that he wasn't okay, and yet a mother had to ask.

"What do you think?" he said, dully.

I know what I lost. His earlier words echoed through her heart. "I think we have to find a way to deal with this," she said, holding her voice steady. Falling apart wouldn't help anyone. Her child needed her to lead.

"I want to go back home."

She knew he was talking about San Antonio. "Abe, that isn't an option. Our life is here now. Our…our life…" She fought the hard lump of emotions. She glanced at Tucker. He didn't say anything, but the edges of his eyes softened and he gave a slight nod of encouragement. She drew strength from his support. Momentarily she wished…what? "Our life will never be the same as it was. But it can be good again. God— Oh, Abe, God *does* have a plan—"

"Yeah, whatever." Abe stood up abruptly on the top rung of the ladder, cutting off her words. He stomped down the rungs. "Let's just go back. No one understands."

"Give it some time. Give the guys a chance. They're a great bunch and they like you."

"Fine, I guess I'm like them, after all."

He looked so lost it hurt. "Dad loved the marines more than me, anyway. I'll meet you at the shop."

"Abe, that's not true."

"Your dad loved you very much, Abe," Tucker spoke up as Abe stalked past him.

"Whatever," Abe said again and kept walking. "It is what it is."

Suzie felt weak watching him go. "How has this happened?" she asked Tucker. "He seemed better, and suddenly he's angrier than ever."

"Grief comes in waves, Suzie, you know that. You've experienced it, I'm sure. But he's really angry at Gordon. And now the boys."

"I know…." She rubbed her forehead, a pain throbbing there. "This seems so raw. So new."

"Has he been angry at Gordon all this time?"

They started walking toward the SUV as Abe disappeared around the edge of the school, heading up the sidewalk. At the rate he was walking, it would take him thirty minutes to make the two blocks to the shop.

"Subconsciously, yes. Me, too. I think— Do you think this could be his hurt coming to the surface finally?" She stopped and turned toward Tucker, raking a hand through her hair in frustration. "The boys of Sunrise Ranch have been abandoned by their families. And I've felt deep down that Abe has felt abandoned by Gordon—though he might not have voiced it in any way but through anger." She paused, the realization coming full force. "I believe being here among them has made him feel like one of them. And he doesn't want to feel like one of them."

"He's fighting it even though he feels that in his heart," Tucker finished for her.

"Does that make sense?" She started walking again, knowing they were on to something. Feeling it deep down.

"Yes, it does." They'd reached the vehicle

and he opened the door for her. "How about you, do you feel that way? Do you feel like Gordon abandoned you? Because he didn't. He loved you too much."

And there it was. "I did. But not now. The emotions are so convoluted. In a situation like this, I guess they all rise to the top."

"I think so. I can give you a counselor's name. She's good and a Christian. This may be something deeper than we can help him with."

"I'll try to talk him into it."

"Y'all will get through this."

"We have to, Tucker. There is no other option."

And there wasn't. Nothing else except Abe getting better was acceptable.

Tucker sat on his porch that night, thinking about Suzie and what she was going through. He'd wanted to take her in his arms and just hold her, she'd looked so alone. As alone as Abe had looked sitting at the top of that slide.

But, as much as he'd wanted to wrap his arms around her, he knew he couldn't. The best thing he could do to offer comfort to Suzie was to help Abe. He'd been surprised at the revelation that the kid was angry with Gordon. Suzie's anger had been at him, not Gordon, and that was what he'd expected from Abe. The abandonment issue had taken him completely by surprise. And that was directly linked to the choice Gordon had made when he took the bullets meant for him.

He felt nauseated thinking about that. Sick in his heart, too.

And all the more certain that he had to fix this.

He'd never backed away from a challenge in his life or a man in need of his help. And he didn't plan on doing it now.

Grief was hard. His mother's death lived with him and always would, but time had helped ease the loss, though he hadn't believed it would as a child. He hadn't bottled it up like Abe. Hadn't had the same issues.

He'd kept silent at the slide that afternoon, letting Suzie take point. But when the time was right he would talk to Abe. He would wait for God to present the right opportunity.

Tucker just needed to be prayed up and ready when that time came. As for Suzie… she'd turned a corner in their relationship by not holding him responsible for Gordon's death. But he needed to remember that there was no room for a relationship between them. He was here to offer help and support where Abe was concerned. Holding her, comforting her, was off-limits. Something between them would only complicate matters and they were already complicated enough.

Still, it was just getting harder and harder to maintain and believe when every fiber in his body wanted something different.

Chapter Eleven

"Stick with the plan."

Suzie said the words out loud as she left for work on Friday morning. She'd come to Dew Drop to start a new life for her and Abe and that was what she planned to do. Being at Sunrise Ranch made more sense to her now than ever.

She needed everyone's support.

"Abe needs it, too," she told herself firmly, her hands tightening on the steering wheel as she gave herself a pep talk. "Staying at the ranch or at least in Dew Drop is for his own good."

Before leaving for work, she'd gone to

the classroom to see Jolie, while the boys finished breakfast. Suzie explained what had happened the day before so Jolie would be aware of what was going on with Abe. Strong and encouraging, Jolie had assured Suzie she would watch out for him and call immediately if something went wrong. And then she'd asked Suzie if they could pray together.

Suzie had needed that connection so much and agreed wholeheartedly. Jolie reaching out to her with prayer lifted Suzie's spirits and was affirmation from God that He was listening. And that she was right where she needed to be, surrounded by an amazing support group.

With her spirits renewed, she walked into her shop and went straight to the phone and called the counselor Tucker had suggested to her. She made herself an appointment. Before she made Abe an appointment, she wanted the doctor's advice.

That done, she got busy.

Today was a full day, with work and then the wedding rehearsal that night. Though she wasn't in the wedding party, Lucy had asked her to be in charge of the wedding book and involved her with the decorating, and so Lucy had insisted she come to the rehearsal dinner.

When she finished work, Suzie would see how Abe's day had gone and decide if she could make the dinner or not.

She felt energized as she worked on the wedding flowers. They had to be extra special for Rowdy and Lucy, and it was a blessing to be busy. As she worked, her thoughts kept going to Abe.

And to Tucker.

He amazed her. That he would continue to stand by her in the face of all the anger she'd harbored toward him spoke of the man he was.

He was strong of character. A man she could lean on, and there had been moments when she'd longed to lean her head against his chest.

Those thoughts she didn't dwell on…. In fact, she moved past them forcibly.

Her life was complicated enough, as it was. She was staying in Dew Drop but Abe was her only concern right now.

Tucker wasn't himself as he headed toward the ranch. He'd missed the wedding rehearsal but knew everyone was eating at the ranch and decorating the barn for the reception.

His day had been a full one. He'd had to go before the monthly grand jury meeting and present several cases. Since the cases were pretty cut-and-dried he felt as though the grand jury would make the indictments so trial dates could be set. One of the cases he'd presented was the wife-abusing tree climber, and Tucker was very proud of the wife for following through with the charges. Sure enough, the jury had indicted the husband.

He'd been on his way back to Dew Drop from the county seat when one of the officers from a nearby community radioed in for backup. Tucker had been close and responded. A situation had evolved into a car chase down a country road with bullets being fired. It'd been dicey there, for a while, but no one was injured.

They could have been, though.

Tucker hadn't had that much action since the marines. He hadn't been prepared for the aftermath…for the flashbacks that had hit him during the gunfire.

Pulling up in front of the barn, he pushed the memories from his mind and exited the truck. Laughter and music filled the air as he approached. In the dusk the glow from the lit-up interior was welcoming. Though he'd really wanted to go home and be alone, he'd known that he needed to show up for Rowdy and Lucy.

Boys were everywhere. Joseph and Wes had a trailer loaded with square hay bales backed to the rear of the building, and they were tossing bales down to the boys, who were stacking them around the barn. Nana was directing them where and how to stack them for seating arrangements and decorations.

At a table in the center of the room stood a group of ladies: Mabel, Ms. Jo, Jolie and Suzie.

With turmoil roiling inside of him, he walked over to say hello and see what he could do to help.

The barn was spotless. It had been cleaned to the point that there was no sign livestock had ever been inside. There was only the fresh scent of the new hay bales being brought in.

"Hey'ya, Tucker," Wes called from his position on the top of the load of hay as he tossed the bales down.

"Hey, yourself, Wes. Looks like the good ol' days of you and Joseph hauling hay all summer."

Joseph grinned affably beside Wes. "Those were some fun times."

"Yup, sure were," Wes agreed, grabbing a square bale as if it was a tin can. "Tony, Jake, Caleb and my boy Abe over there held their own loading this stuff up today."

Joseph gave a thumbs-up. "That's right."

"You two relax. You've got great backup taking up the slack, and we're really proud of them. Couldn't run the place without your dedication or theirs."

"That's what I'm talkin' about," Wes said. "My dudes are making me proud."

Tucker gave them a tip of his hat, not missing that Abe didn't look at him. At least he'd pitched in and was helping. Hanging out with the guys was the best thing for him.

Morgan came in and set a box down.

"Missed you at the rehearsal. Must have been bad."

Tucker had called Morgan to let him know he wasn't going to make it to the church on time. "Yeah, it was. I'll fill you in later. You'll make sure I know what I'm doing tomorrow, right?"

Morgan grinned. "I don't know, it's pretty hard to walk out there and stand beside your brother. Then watch a string of pretty ladies and a beautiful bride come strolling down the aisle."

Tucker had to chuckle at that. "Yeah, I was afraid things might have changed in the months since your wedding."

"Nope, still the same. You'll be fine. Come help unload the boxes of decorations from my truck. I've never seen so much stuff. The gals must have been warehousing this stuff over at Lucy's studio."

"Be right there. Let me say hello to the women."

"Sure, just don't let them snare you into helping till we finish unloading the truck." He laughed and headed back out the rear door.

Tucker didn't stay long saying hi to the

ladies. They were chattering like a bunch of magpies anyway, laughing and having a great time. Suzie was gathering a bunch of greenery wrapped with lights and she stepped away from the table as he walked toward her. She looked beautiful, and though she appeared to be smiling and in good spirits, he thought he could detect worry creasing the edges of her eyes.

He wanted to talk to her, ask her how her day went and how Abe had done. He wanted to hold her in his arms—he broke that thought off. "Are you about to hang that somewhere?" he asked, spotting the tall ladder in the center of the room.

"She's about to climb that thing," Ms. Jo called. "You showed up just in time, Tucker. Climb that ladder and hang that garland for her, please."

"Oh, that is a perfect thing for you to do," Mabel added, smiling like an opossum. "And you stay over there and make sure he gets it done right, Suzie. You know these men don't know the first thing about decorating with flowers and such."

Tucker wasn't unhappy at all about the opportunity to spend time with Suzie. "I'd be glad to do that. You ladies just tell me what to do."

The tension coiled inside of him eased as he and Suzie walked toward the ladder. She glanced at him, studying him for a minute. "You've had a hard day."

It wasn't a question and he shrugged it off; suddenly, looking at her, everything seemed better. "It had its tough spots. But it all turned out good." And it had. It hadn't turned out like the day Gordon died, despite the flashbacks that had hit him as the bullets flew past.

"Maybe, after we decorate, you can tell me about it if you need to talk. You've tried so hard to help me, it would be nice to repay the kindness."

They just looked at each other for a moment. "How's Abe today?" he asked, after a beat or two. "I see he's helping with the hay."

"Jolie said he was silent during class. That he didn't participate, but he wasn't rude. I'm worried about him, but he was helping Wes and Joseph with the hay when I got here and I thought that was a good sign."

"It can't hurt. So, what do you want me to do with this stuff?" he asked, reaching to take it from her hands. Their fingers touched.

"We're wrapping it around those beams, so it's going to take a little time. Are you sure you have time to do this? I'm not afraid of a ladder."

"I'm here to help. But you will have to direct me or there is no telling what it will look like."

She chuckled, and the sound sent his pulse racing. "I'll stay close. Don't worry."

He nodded and climbed the ladder as fast as he could. He liked the thought of her staying close far too much to linger beside her listening to her laughter.

The evening had passed by quickly and Suzie stared at how lovely the barn looked. The garland was hung from the rafters, thanks to Tucker and Morgan, who'd been roped into joining in as soon as he'd looked as though he had nothing to do. It had been a fun experience listening to him and Tucker complain to each other, teasing the women with their moaning and groaning.

As soon as the boys had finished unloading the hay, they'd gone off and she'd lost track of Abe, though she'd relaxed a little during the evening seeing him interact with the boys. She just had to give it time. She couldn't panic, and she couldn't pull up stakes and move just because he wanted her to.

She was standing by the stables after waving good-night to everyone. The younger boys had been gathered up earlier by their house parents and taken to their homes on the ranch. The older boys had a later curfew on Friday night and were hanging out at the end of the arena under the lights, riding and cutting up. She could spot Abe and prayed that today had been good for him. She planned to talk to him before he went to bed.

She was standing in the shadows watching the boys, and remained there for a few minutes, not ready to go in just yet. She told herself she wasn't lingering to talk to Tucker before he headed home, but she wasn't convinced that was the truth. He'd gone into the stables with his dad and Pepper earlier and she wondered how long they would be. She got her answer soon when they emerged, all smiles. They greeted her, then Pepper waved and headed to his truck.

"Rowdy brought in a few new horses today," Randolph said. "They're beauties. You should get Tucker to show them to you. I'm heading to bed. Got to get my beauty sleep, you know." He gave her a quick hug before leaving. His home was elsewhere on the ranch, as Morgan's and Rowdy's were.

Suddenly she found herself alone with Tucker. He looked so handsome in the moonlight. She'd known just by looking at him earlier that something had happened at work. Something stressful. She knew it had been important if he missed the rehearsal because of it.

But now, he seemed more relaxed. Still she'd been curious about what had happened. Had it been dangerous?

"Do you want to see the colts?"

"Sure, I'd love that."

He smiled. "Then follow me."

Single bulbs down the center of the alleyway lit the stable, and they glowed bright as they entered. Soft nickers came from the stalls as they walked toward the tack room on the right, down a few stalls to where a beautiful tan horse stood watching them. It was the color of caramel with a vanilla mane and huge chocolate eyes.

"How gorgeous," Suzie said, loving the color.

"This is Bow. He's going to be as good a cutting horse as he is beautiful once Rowdy finishes training him. And this next big fella is Cisco, and we have high hopes for him, too."

Cisco was coffee-brown with black eyes and he jerked his head up and down, as if nodding agreement. Suzie laughed at the sight. "Hey, boy," she said to him. "You're a confident fella. I like that."

He nickered and pawed his foot on the ground. Tucker chuckled beside her, and she was suddenly very aware of how close they were standing. Her pulse skipped.

"I think he's going to be competitive," she said, running her hand down the side of his neck, which had Bow sticking his head over his stall gate and nudging her shoulder for some loving. "Okay, didn't mean to leave you out, handsome. You're both going to be competitive and confident."

Tucker was watching her with a thoughtful smile. "They like you. They haven't been this friendly to anyone. Rowdy may have you out here helping him if you're not careful."

"I think I'll stick to flower arranging. No offense, boys," she added, giving each horse one last rub on the nose. "This barn is really old, isn't it? I mean, I think I heard your nana talking about it to someone."

"Yeah, it is. My great-great-grandfather built it back in the early 1900s. We've diligently taken care of it over the years. Those harnesses hanging on the back wall over there are antiques, too.

"Come here and I'll show you the saddles." He opened the door to the tack room and flipped on a light.

Suzie entered first. It was a long room with saddle racks along both sides of the room. On a ranch with this many boys, one expected there to be a lot of saddles and there were. "Wow!" she gasped. "That is amazing. How many of them are there?"

Tucker moved into the narrow room with her, and when she looked up at him, butterflies immediately erupted in her chest.

"There's about thirty in this room," Tucker said, holding her gaze before looking back at the saddle. "One for each boy and then everyone else's. We have a separate place for the hands to store theirs. But these aren't what I was going to show you. It's those at the back."

"Oh." Suzie was flustered by the way she was reacting and moved quickly toward the back wall, putting space between them.

On the back wall were six saddles, three on the bottom row and three sitting on wall-mounted racks above the bottom three. It was clear these weren't regular saddles. The tooling on them was too fancy and there were also things written on them.

"These were my grandfather's, my great-grandfather's and my great-great-grandfather's and grandmother's saddles."

"Oh, wow, they are amazing."

"Yeah, it shows how, given a little tender loving care, things last. The initials TRM on this one here stand for Tucker Randolph McDermott, who was my great-great-granddad. This saddle is actually mine now. I just can't bring myself to take it out of the place it's always set, so I leave it here to remind the boys of the roots this place has."

"I wouldn't be able to take it from here, either." She ran her fingertips over the smooth leather. "Abe hanging out with the guys today was a good sign," she said, glancing at him, "I think he's going to get over this abandonment issue, just like I have." She couldn't look away from him.

Tucker touched her then; he lifted his hand and cupped her jaw gently. "I think so. Whatever you need, I'm here. I'm glad we're talking now, like this."

She nodded, fighting the urge to close her eyes and enjoy the warmth of his touch. A noise outside the open door broke the moment and she smiled, stepping away. "Thank you. I think it's going to be much better for Abe. I guess I'd better go in now."

"Right," he agreed, tucking the hand that had been cupping her jaw into the front pocket of his jeans. "I'll go check on the boys. It's time for even the older fellas to turn in. I'll send Abe your way."

"Great. I'd appreciate that." She was moving fast now—needing space between them. She was not comfortable with the way his touch melted her mind and made her respond.

"Talk to you tomorrow," she said, and left him there. It took resolve on her part not to jog across the lot to the porch.

Not being angry and blaming Tucker for

Gordon's death created a new problem. It allowed the attraction she'd been fighting to gain footing.

What was she going to do about that?

Chapter Twelve

Tucker wasn't in the best of moods when he woke the next morning. He was in trouble and he knew it. He was falling for Suzie, and he wasn't at all sure how to handle that.

Gordon weighed heavy on his mind all night. The guilt weighed heaviest—despite accepting that his friend was a marine, just as he was, and accepted the risk and responsibility that came with taking that oath.

He was in his SUV heading to the office when his cell phone rang. "Good morning, Pepper," he said, having seen the caller ID.

"Tucker, you need to get back out here,"

Pepper demanded, not bothering to greet him. "We've got problems here in the horse barn."

He could hear the seriousness in his friend's voice. "What's going on?"

"You just need to get out here and don't tell anyone why until you meet me at the barn. I need to show you something in the tack room." Tucker started to say he'd just been there last night but Pepper wasn't one to make demanding, ominous remarks so Tucker didn't waste time, instead he made a quick U-turn and pressed the gas.

He walked into the barn a few minutes later, managing to avoid being stopped by anyone as he arrived. Pepper was waiting.

"What's up, Pepper?"

He shook his head. "You're not gonna like it." He led the way to the tack room and unlocked it. He never locked the tack room. That room had been unlocked for all of Tucker's life.

"I got here at sunup and saw the door open. The boys know the rules."

The rule being that no matter what—the door to the tack room was *always* closed to protect the saddles and the other gear. Tucker replayed the night before, knowing he'd shut the door securely when he and Suzie had left. It had been nearly eleven o'clock by that time.

Pepper looked over his shoulder. "This is what I found." He pushed open the door and let Tucker inside. Pepper slipped in and closed the door behind them.

Tucker's heart jerked, his trained eye instantly going to the back wall. His saddle, the one that had belonged to his great-great-granddad, had been destroyed. It was spray-painted red and black, and the discarded spray cans had been thrown on the ground beside it.

From where Tucker stood at the far end of the room, it didn't look as though anything could repair the ruined handcrafted leather.

His great-great-grandfather had hand-tooled the designs himself, the hours and hours of labor and artistry now destroyed. Unless something could remove the paint it was ruined, but even then it would never be the same.

Tucker's mouth went dry; the heat of anger swept through him like a grassfire. Swift and charring.

"I'm sorry, Tucker."

Tucker had to clear the lump out of his throat. "Not your fault, Pepper." He forced himself to walk the endless length of the room to the saddle. Close up, it was as bad as he'd thought. Vandalism at its highest. The letters TRM were filled with paint so thick that even the groove where Great-great-granddad Tucker had dug his tool into the leather was almost invisible.

Unless the culprit had worn gloves, the cans at his feet would make identifying the responsible party easy—if his fingerprints were on record. Tucker seriously doubted gloves had been worn. But he knew it didn't matter. He knew who had done this.

This was the work of an angry teen. And Tucker hated it, hated thinking what he was thinking, and knowing with certainty in his heart who the prints would reveal.

Abe wasn't getting better, as Suzie hoped.

"Who else has seen this, Pepper?"

"No one, I don't think. I locked it up right after I found it and called you." Pepper had worked at the ranch since being hired on as a teen by Tucker's granddad in the early years when he'd first started the ranch. He knew the sentimental value that saddle held for Tucker. "There is a lot of hurt in this."

"Yeah. I know I don't have to tell you, but we need to keep this to ourselves for right now."

"I figured as much, for more reasons than one. I'm thinking Rowdy and Lucy's wedding doesn't need to be marred by this, if possible."

"Exactly. And the other is, I need to get the prints."

"Not that you need the prints if my, and I'm sure your, suspicion is correct?"

Pepper knew the boys, and had seen every kid who'd come through Sunrise Ranch since its inception. He was a keen observer of behavior—both of human and horse. Not much got by him and that was why the wise older cowboy was such a valuable asset to the ranch. Tucker laid a hand on his shoulder. "I need some time. I'll do an official investigation and gather evidence, then we can clean this up and no one will be the wiser. Till then, the door stays locked. No one is going to need a saddle out of here till after the wedding, anyway."

"You got it," Pepper said, as they slipped out and he locked up behind them.

Tucker left; he needed to think. He'd learned what was valuable in life and it wasn't things acquired, whether they were sentimental or valuable. He'd live, even though he hated what had been done to the antique. The question was—what was the best thing to be done for Abe? And though a man was considered innocent till proven guilty, Tucker had good instincts honed from years of experience and this had Abe written all over it.

The church looked absolutely beautiful, but it didn't even compare to Lucy as she stood in the doorway beside her father as the wedding music began. Suzie had come to love the beautiful blonde in the short time they'd known each other.

"She looks like a princess doll," B.J. said, the moment he spotted Lucy standing in the door of the church.

"Wow," Sammy echoed beside him.

Wes leaned forward. "Shhh, hold it down, little dudes. You're going to make Rowdy jealous." He chuckled, and Suzie and everyone else did, too.

Rowdy was so handsome in his black suit.

His white shirt set off his jet-black hair and that dazzling smile was as large as it could get. His eyes twinkled watching Lucy. She practically floated down the aisle toward him.

She did look like a fairy princess meeting her prince. The music came to a halt as she and her father reached the front of the church. Beside Rowdy, Tucker and Morgan looked just as handsome.

Jolie was Lucy's bridesmaid, and her best friend from school had flown in to be her maid of honor. Kimberly had gleaming blond hair and her emerald eyes kept roaming to Tucker. Since she and Lucy had gone to dinner last night with Lucy's parents, and since Tucker had missed the rehearsal, they hadn't met until just before the wedding.

Suzie took Kimberly's immediate infatuation with Tucker as a sure sign she'd been right. Tucker affected all women the way he affected her. It made her feel better.

Somewhat. Thoughts of standing beside him in the tack room had her confused.

Pushing those thoughts away, she concentrated on the ceremony. Lucy's father had given her away and now Rowdy had taken her hand and led her to stand before the preacher.

Watching the sweet ceremony, Suzie's heart swelled and she prayed they would live a long and happy life together. She prayed for a happy ever after for them.

"Are they married yet?" B.J. hissed, looking over his shoulder at Wes. "Can I whoop?"

The preacher chuckled, since there was no use pretending that everyone hadn't heard his loud whisper. "Not yet, son, hold your horses."

That got laughter everywhere.

"Hey, I'm just as anxious as he is." Rowdy grinned at B.J., then winked at Lucy.

The pastor went on to tell how God had created marriage and what a sacred union it was between a man and a woman. And then he pronounced them man and wife.

Rowdy almost kissed Lucy before the preacher told him to. Suzie misted up with tenderness, she was so happy for them.

Feeling a gentle prick of awareness, her gaze shifted, and there was Tucker watching her. As her eyes met his he gave a slight lift to his lips and then the music started and he moved to offer his arm to Kimberly. The boys were clapping and whooping and hooting as Rowdy and Lucy headed toward the doors. Then came Tucker and Kimberly— who was smiling up at him as if he'd just slayed dragons for her.

Jolie and Morgan came striding by next, looking like the perfect couple. From the front row, Nana had turned to watch everyone leave.

Did Suzie's expression convey some of the internal turmoil being around Tucker threw her into? She'd never been able to hide her feelings well, but in this instance it was purely about crazy, mixed-up emotions that even she didn't understand.

Or didn't want to understand.

The words echoed in the back of her thoughts, disturbing yet...completely true.

Tucker stood to the side of the barn, watching the festivities. Rowdy and Lucy were dancing their first dance to Clint Black's duet with his wife, Lisa Hartman Black, "When I Said I Do." They looked so happy. It was as if no one else was in the room.

He was glad for them, though as the evening wore down, his mood was growing darker and darker. Suzie looked beautiful, and she was avoiding him. Not to mention that Lucy's friend was a really nice woman, but it had taken him half the night to politely extract himself from her company.

As Tucker visited with relatives and friends his gaze kept finding Suzie in the crowd. She was having a good evening and he was glad he'd chosen to keep the vandalism hidden until after the wedding. Everyone deserved to loosen up a little and that went double for Suzie. She'd know soon enough what Abe had done, but she wouldn't know it until he had absolute proof.

Raking his hands through his hair, he wondered if his life could get any more complicated.

Suzie kept her distance from him and had been busy helping with the reception, so that made it easy. But when he saw her slip out the side door, he was immediately torn, wanting to follow her and make sure she was okay.

The tension he'd been feeling all day wound tighter inside of him. After a moment, he made the decision and slipped out the side door, too.

The cool night enveloped him—one of those perfect summer nights two people could get lost in. The moon washed everything in a silvery glow that elongated shadows and promised romance.

He fought that thought. His frustration twisting tighter, he scanned the landscape, searching for Suzie. It almost seemed that you could see a mile in the moon's glow.

Behind him in the barn, Clint and Lisa's song finished and the live band took over with another slow romantic ballad. Spotting Suzie's silhouette over at the rear of the horse barn beside the round pens, his gut twisted as he headed that way. He just needed to check on her and make sure she was all right, he told himself.

"Suzie," he called softly, with twenty feet to go before reaching her, not wanting to startle her.

"Hi," she said, glancing over her shoulder. She remained where she was, with her elbows resting on the railing, watching the colts playing in the moonlight in the center of the arena.

He moved to stand beside her. "Everything okay?"

She took a deep breath and didn't look

at him. He placed his elbows on the railing, too.

"It was a beautiful wedding."

"Yes, it was. Like I said, my brothers are lucky men."

"I think so, too. Jolie and Lucy are wonderful."

"I consider Gordon my brother, too. He was a lucky man, also."

She slanted her head toward him. "I'm glad he had this amazing place to grow up in. He never really talked about his family life before the ranch, but I know it wasn't good. He preferred to talk about the ranch and all of you."

"Most of the boys don't talk about their past. When the pain of rejection eases after they arrive, and the joy of living seeps into them, they choose not to talk about it."

She took that in silently. "And yet they still hurt some, don't they?"

"Sure they do. Our past never leaves us. You and I know that. It stays with us forever. But we learn to live with the scars. To share space with them. The good and the bad." He let his words sink in. "Wes and Joseph have moved on and are seeking their own lives. They've come to peace with their lives. I sometimes believe that Wes is still slaying memories that haunt him. He has a rage that hides inside him despite the joy you see…. A little like Abe."

"But Wes is so happy," she said, before he could move on. "I wouldn't think he was still fighting his past."

"Sometimes what you see on the outside isn't what is truly going on inside. Wes, he's always been a great cheerleader for the boys and will make you laugh at the drop of a hat, but he's fighting something. He chooses to fight it alone. Something I'm hoping Abe will choose not to do."

Suzie turned her back to the arena and leaned against the bars, studying him across one shoulder. He moved toward her, the soft, sweet scent of her drawing him. She wore a sleeveless pale apricot dress that shimmered against her skin in the soft light. She was radiant in the moonlight. And his thinking got fuzzy when he looked into her eyes.

"And Joseph, what a sweet guy."

Tucker had to focus. "Joseph is. They don't get any better than that kid." Tucker didn't want to talk about the boys. His gaze dropped to her lips and he fought the strong need to kiss her. Her skin looked so silky in the golden light.

"You're a nice guy, too, Tucker." The words were soft, and the she probably wished she hadn't said them the moment they crossed her pretty lips. But they meant the world to him.

She would never know how deep they went. "I try. Strong and dependable are what I strive for."

"I…" She started to say something but the words trailed off.

They were both caught in an invisible force that seemed unshakable. He touched her shoulder ever so lightly, traced the curve, and held her gaze. Fighting every instinct inside of him to maintain his distance, it all went out the window when she shifted slightly toward him, as if drawn to him. Leaning forward, he hesitated for a second, holding her gaze, then touched his lips to hers.

Time stalled.

His hand came up under her chin, lifting it slightly as she stepped into the shadow of his body.

The kiss was gentle, a prelude to what could be between them, and bittersweet at the same moment because of what couldn't be. But for a brief moment he felt freedom and peace...and promise.

Reality slammed into him full force.

He pulled away, knowing that even if Suzie gave in to this right now, in this moment, beneath the romance of the sky and the soft music from the wedding reception, she would feel as though it was a mistake.

Grabbing the arena rails, he turned to stare at the colts once more.

Every nerve in his body hummed with the need to pull her close, to wrap her fully in his embrace and kiss her soundly…and freely. But that would never happen.

She had turned back to the horses, too. "I don't know what this is. There is too much past."

Tucker closed his eyes, her words sank in deeper. "Gordon was a marine and a good one. The burden of his death is hard on me, but I only take it to a point. After that point, though, it was his choice. Taking that away wrongs him, Suzie. You said it yourself the other day at the playground. It steals some of the pride he had for his country and the sacrifice he was willing to make for it. For you and Abe. It's unjust." He ground the last words out with stern assurance and knew the truth at last. Knew he could no longer steal that from his brother-in-arms. It wasn't his to steal. "Gordon would have done what he did for any of his unit. It wasn't about me, Suzie." The truth hit him in that moment. It was raw and powerful, and it was freeing.

He turned to stare into Suzie's eyes. "It wasn't about me." He almost laughed, he felt so free in that moment. "Gordon was my brother and I hated what happened. But I'm letting go, Suzie, because he didn't give his life for me. He gave it for his fellow marine—his marine brother. He would have done it for anyone in that unit."

She stared at him, and he realized that he'd taken her by the arms sometime in the past minute. He gently tugged her toward him again, hugging her with relief. "You felt what I felt when I kissed you."

"Tucker, this is all too soon."

"This is not just a fleeting infatuation and you know it."

"Tucker, I've just stopped resenting you. This…" She waved her hand between them, having backed out of his arms. "This is too soon. I'm not ready."

"Not ready or scared?"

Her brows dipped. "Both. Yes, I feel this, this electricity that hums between us, just as well as you do."

He smiled at that admission. "Do you, now?"

Her eyes flashed. "Don't tease me. This is important."

"Oh, it's important. Believe me, I know that. I've felt this bond with you from day one and denied it. But after that kiss, whether it should have happened or not, there is no more denying. Suzie, that kiss gave me clarity to see through the fog of guilt. I see the truth. So you know how important that was for me? Life changing."

She backed a step away from him. "I came here for Abe. I can't get involved with you or anyone right now. Abe couldn't handle it."

The saddle vandalism. How had he forgotten about that? He'd been too caught up in the emotions of the moment.

"I can only think about Abe right now," she said, her eyes full of turmoil. Spinning away, she hurried back toward the barn and the festivities.

Tucker started to go after her, every instinct wanted to. Instead he watched her leave. He needed time to think.

He'd been an idiot kissing her.

What had he thought it would accomplish?

That was the problem… He hadn't thought at all.

He'd brought his fingerprint kit and now was the perfect time to put his mind where it belonged and take fingerprints and evidence from the tack room. Was it what he wanted to be doing? No. He wanted to be kissing Suzie.

Not finding out if her son had destroyed a family memory.

Chapter Thirteen

Two days after the wedding, Suzie had orders for a funeral flooding in and it kept her busy. She needed to be busy. Though she hated that the poor man had passed away, that was the nature of her business. She just had to do it to the best of her ability so that her flowers gave joy or comfort in someone's time of need. It was the aspect of the business that she loved.

Abe had continued to be distant and aloof, though he was spending every minute he wasn't in school with Wes and Joseph. She kept thinking about what Tucker had said about Wes and prayed that Wes might have a good influence on Abe. The door opened and Chili stuck his head in. "Place is looking good."

"Thanks, Chili. Have you come for another flower arrangement?"

He got a hound-dog expression. "Ha! Ruby won't hardly talk to me these days."

Drewbaker stepped in beside him. "She sure won't. I told him to send her another arrangement, but he's chicken."

"I'm not falling for that again."

"Well, Nana's a nice lady. I'm sure time will heal this situation."

She thought about her own situation with Tucker. Things had gotten so complicated.

Drewbaker got a twinkle in his eyes. "True love always finds a way is what I told him."

Suzie chuckled. "You two are a mess. I meant to tell you that I enjoyed your fiddle and banjo playing with the band."

They beamed and the conversation switched to their music. Suzie had learned to just keep on working when they came by or she might not get any work done. Today she enjoyed the distraction they gave her from thinking about Tucker.

However, as soon as they walked out the door, five minutes didn't pass before Tucker came walking in.

She hadn't forgotten their kiss. She didn't think she would ever forget it.

"Suzie, we need to talk," he said, before he had the door closed. His tone alerted her instantly.

"What's wrong?"

He placed a manila envelope on the counter. She glanced from it to him.

"What's this?"

His expression grim, he pushed the envelope toward her. "It's about Abe."

She felt the color drain from her face and her stomach turn over. Tucker wouldn't look so disturbed if this wasn't something bad. She knew him well and while she had no control over her expressions, he was the opposite.

"What's in that?" She wanted to recoil. Foreboding hung like the stench of bad eggs in the air.

"You need to look at this." His gaze shifted, turning amazingly tender.

She inhaled a shaky breath, disturbed even more.

"It's going to be all right, Suzie. But you need to see these pictures and then we'll come up with a plan. Together."

She needed to sit down, but refused to give in to the weakness. She picked the envelope up and lifted the flap.

"What?" The word came out weakly as she pulled them out. There were five photos. Fingers shaking, she spread them on the counter.

They were of what had once been a beautiful saddle. It had been ruined with red and black spray paint, every inch a motley mixture of offensive coating. She swallowed the lump in her throat; it refused to go away. She didn't want to look at Tucker. Didn't want to see what she knew she was going to see in his eyes. The truth—but she had to. His eyes were full of compassion when she finally lifted hers to meet his.

"Please tell me this wasn't Abe."

His lips flattened together, momentarily locked, as if he didn't want to tell her. "I took fingerprints before I could talk to you. I'm sorry, but they belong to Abe."

She grasped the edge of the counter for support. "When? When did he do this?"

"The night that I showed the saddles to you. Pepper found it like this when he came to work that morning."

She closed her eyes, not wanting to believe it. "Wait. You *knew* this the night of the wedding?"

"I knew, but I didn't know who. I had my suspicions, but no proof."

"And you didn't tell me? You kissed

me! Instead of telling me something this important—"

"I know you're angry at me for that. That wasn't meant to happen. But this isn't about me kissing you, Suzie." He waved at the photos. "This is separate. This is about Abe."

"And you think I'm not aware of that." She fought the urge to snatch the vase and throw it against the wall. She never threw things.

"His fingerprints are all over everything." Tucker inhaled heavily. "There is a lot of anger here. Suzie, this was directed at me. You can't tell it in this picture but that is the saddle with TRM engraved on it."

"No," she gasped, her hand going to her heart as the sentimental value of this heirloom dawned. "I'm so sorry. It was priceless."

"It was. But it's not the saddle itself that matters, it's why he chose this saddle, my saddle, out of those sitting there. I don't believe that was a random act."

She shook her head. "No. I don't believe it was. Remember that noise we heard? Do you think he overheard us talking? Maybe looked in and saw us?"

"Those are my same suspicions. I think he heard me talking about the initials and knew that was my saddle. No one but Pepper knows about this. He discovered it and called me, keeping it locked up until I could gather the evidence."

At the word *evidence* Suzie couldn't stop the tears. Couldn't stop the dam that broke. This was San Antonio all over again.

Tucker watched her tears flow, wanting to pull Suzie into his arms but knowing she didn't want him to. He'd really messed up kissing her before they'd made it through the trouble facing them. And now he couldn't even console her.

Couldn't console the woman he loved.

The truth settled over him with the ease of rightness. Rightness for him, but not for Suzie.

"Look at me, Suzie," he said, gently. "This is going to be all right. There was anger and vandalism here, but not real violence. He just expressed his frustration. If I believed differently I'd suggest radical steps. But I've seen a lot in my life and this isn't the end of the world. I know it feels like it to you. And I knew that when I had to come and tell you, and that was why I dreaded it. Still, it's not the end of the world. It's time for action."

"I've called the therapist." She dried her tears. Took a deep breath and nodded. "I was going to talk to her myself first. But I'll call her and tell her what has happened and see what she thinks I should do. If she says bring him in before she sees me first, then that's what I'll do."

"I'll talk to the counselor with you if you need me."

"Thank you. But I can do it."

He put the photos back in the envelope and closed it. "Okay, but let me know if I can help. I'm not pursuing this officially."

"Thank you." She crossed her arms, hugging herself. As if giving herself comfort that he longed to give her. "I'm fine. I better call her now."

Feeling lousy, he gave a short nod and left.

He had to find a way to fix this, but he was feeling out of control. And he had never done out of control well.

As he was climbing into his SUV he caught sight of Drewbaker and Chili sitting on the church pew. Both of them were grinning like hyenas and giving him a thumbs-up.

Crazy old fellas—if they only knew.

Chapter Fourteen

Suzie dried her tears after Tucker left and called the counselor. She was done crying. And she was done letting her son get away with something so wrong. That saddle was irreplaceable. After talking with the counselor she hung up, locked the door and went to the ranch.

She couldn't get over how understanding Tucker had been. It was amazing, really.

When she pulled into the yard and got out, she scanned the area looking for Abe.

B.J. spotted her and came hurrying toward her. "Hi, Suzie. You lookin' for your boy?"

Sweet kid. "Yes, I am. Have you seen

him?" She gave him a hug and he returned it fiercely. He smelled of sweaty little boy and she was reminded of Abe at the age of eight. Oh, how life was simpler then. But that was then and this was now, and she had to stop wishing for the way things had been.

And so did Abe.

"He's mucking out stalls."

"Thanks, little man." She winked at him and headed that way.

"You're a nice momma."

She turned back at B.J.'s words. "Oh, thank you. You're a nice boy."

He giggled. "Thanks. I got to run. I got trash duty today."

She watched him race toward the chow hall. Then she headed toward the stables just as Abe was coming out.

"Hi, Abe, I need you to come with me," she said, firmly.

"Where?"

"I'll tell you on the way. Come on."

"I don't want to go."

She looked at him. "Abe, I didn't ask you." He stared at her and she held her gaze steady. There was a time to be firm and this was it. Making decisions alone had been hard. And she had to admit that there had been times when it was easier not to push issues. But that time had passed.

"Get in the car, Abe. Now."

His eyes flashed, but he did as she asked. Stomping to the other side of the car, he yanked open the door and slouched in the car seat.

"Buckle up," she said, as she got in. "We have a long drive."

He sat up then. "Are we going back home?"

She started the car and backed out. "No, Abe, this is our home now. And it's time you got used to that. Now buckle up."

He yanked the seat belt over and buck-led it.

"I'm not sure if you thought destroying Tucker's saddle was going to make me give in and take you back to San Antonio. I'm not sure what you were thinking when you did such a horrible thing. But I can tell you that some things are going to change, Abe Kent. And the first thing is that you're going to see a counselor."

"I don't want to see a shrink!"

She turned onto the blacktop and kept her eyes on the road. She knew his expression wouldn't be good. "She's nice, Abe. She'll listen to anything you have to say. Anything you need to talk about that is bothering you. But you have to open up. You have to let go of what is eating at you."

"I'm not talking."

She glanced at him. "I'll take you anyway. You can sit in her office, silent for every appointment, but you'll be there anyway. This has to stop. And you will not manipulate me into giving you what you want through bad behavior."

Was she doing this the right way? She didn't know, but one thing she did know was that giving in and being soft hadn't worked. She'd been so thankful when Dr. Livingston had said she did evening appointments and she'd had a cancellation. It had clearly been a gift from God, and she'd grabbed the opportunity immediately.

Still, the miles ticked by slowly after that. He didn't speak and she felt it best to not push any more. This was for his own good. She decided the time would be better spent in prayer.

For both of them.

Moonlight cast Tucker's front yard in a silvery glow. Alone, in shadow of his porch, he was still reeling from the afternoon in Suzie's shop. He was free. Despite every doubt and every feeling of guilt and remorse he'd carried over the past two years, he was finally free of it. Free because he'd realized finally that Gordon had done what he had to do—that it hadn't been about giving his life for Tucker but instead about honoring the oath he'd taken when he'd become a marine.

The pain was still there, the wish that he could turn back time and change what had happened. But the burden that he'd carried was no longer there.

But where did that leave him with Suzie? Did that mean he was free to want Suzie? Because he did.

He wanted her in his life and he wanted her to want him…to want a life with him. To love him. But was that a possibility? Was he free to want that?

Gordon had been his brother—maybe not by blood but he was by everything else that counted. His mind kept looping back to kissing Suzie in the moonlight. Those thoughts had brought him outside to sit on his porch, letting the calm of the night seep in as he let everything settle in his thoughts.

She wasn't ready for a relationship and

he understood that. They had to help Abe first. He understood that and wanted that.

But he also understood what he wanted. And despite the misgivings, he'd fallen for Suzie.

Understood that he loved Suzie and he'd do anything for her. He could only hope that she might return his feelings someday, given time.

Just as had been the plan all along, their priority was Abe. But, from here on out, Suzie was going to know that she was special. That she wasn't alone.

When his phone rang, he glanced at the caller ID fully expecting it to be the dispatcher at the office. He was startled when he realized it was Suzie calling at eleven-thirty. Grabbing the phone up from the table, he punched the button, his heart kicking up a ruckus. "Suzie, everything okay?"

She hesitated. "Tucker." Her voice was quiet. "Can we talk?"

He sat up. "Sure."

"I mean in person."

"Of course. I'll be right there. Meet me on the porch in ten minutes."

"Okay, thank you."

"Anytime."

Her voice had been so soft, so full of the weight of concern, that he knew this was about Abe. But she'd called, and that mattered a great deal to him.

Heading back into the house, he pulled on a T-shirt with his jeans, yanked on his boots and jogged down the steps to his truck, opting for his personal vehicle instead of his official SUV. He was actually not on duty for three days. He was off all weekend unless there was a major catastrophe.

Within the ten minutes he'd allotted himself, he was driving into the yard of the ranch and pulling to a halt in front of the porch. He stepped lightly as he walked up the steps, not sure if Suzie was already outside sitting in the shadows.

"Hey," came her sweet voice from the swing.

"Hey, yourself," he said, continuing to keep his steps quiet, not wanting to disturb anyone inside. "Mind if I sit down?"

She shook her head and he sank into the cushion on the porch swing beside her. Her hair was still damp from her shower and she wore an oversize green T-shirt with a pair of black lounging pants. Her legs were tucked in between them, and her bare feet peeked from beneath the hem of her pants. She looked comfortable and relaxed, but her expression was pinched and her eyes weary.

He laid a comforting hand on her calf, patting gently before laying his arm across the back of the swing. "How are you? What's on your mind?"

She took a deep breath. "A lot. I called the counselor right after you left and she was so accommodating. She had an evening appointment open and urged me to bring Abe in to see her. So I came to the ranch and basically demanded Abe come with me. He wasn't happy, but he got in the car and I took him."

"Sometimes, you have to be firm. I know, if you're worried about the emotional state of your child that makes it all the more difficult." He toyed with a damp strand of her hair. "Not that I have parenting experience—"

"Working with all these boys at the ranch gives you more experience than I have. Don't kid yourself. I value your experience."

He gave her hair a gentle tug. "Thanks. I want to help and I'm glad the doc could see y'all. How was it?"

"Well, I told Abe before we got there that his bad behavior wouldn't be rewarded. That this was our home and that we would not be going back to San Antonio, no matter how much he acted up. After I said that, he didn't talk to me the rest of the hour-long drive to the appointment."

She worried a spot on the swing's arm— rubbing on it and thinking. "When we were in with Dr. Livingston and I brought up the saddle, he just crossed his arms, closing us out, and stared out the window."

"That's tough."

"Yeah, but Dr. Livingston didn't act like it was uncommon." Suzie sighed. "Abe didn't talk for thirty minutes. Just sat there. Dr. Livingston started talking to me, explaining that she'd asked us both in there tonight, but that on the other trips she would see Abe alone. Toward the end of the session she did ask me to step out and she spent a short time alone with him. I think to see if he had anything to say when I wasn't in the room. I'm not certain, but he may have talked a little with her."

"How is he now? Or on the ride home?"

"He was quiet." She looked at him then. "But I think he was resolved. Hopefully he understands that I care, and this is for his own good. I told him that, and maybe some of it is getting through. And hopefully he knows he's going to have to accept that Sunrise Ranch—I mean, Dew Drop is his home."

"Sunrise Ranch is okay, it is his home."

"No, actually, it isn't, Tucker. That's one of the things I wanted to talk to you about. This has been wonderful as a temporary layover. And he will continue to go to school out here, but I need to make a home for him so that he feels like we're a family again. Because the truth is, he isn't exactly like all of these wonderful boys here. He does still have a mother who cares for him. He hasn't been abandoned by both his parents. I hate that so much for the boys, that they have, but Abe hasn't. And this has made me more than realize that we need our own place. I can bring him to school each morning, and he can stay and hang out, work on the ranch whatever needs to be done. But at night he'll go home to his own bed in his own room."

"Okay, I get it. He really may need that separation. So, what can I do to help?"

"Well, I'm going upstairs to the apartment in the morning and I'm going to start cleaning and arranging. It shouldn't take me long at all. We'll start there, and then, that will keep him close. It will give him a place to call home. I hope that doesn't hurt any feelings, but at the moment this is about Abe."

"That's fine. You're absolutely right. In the meantime, I'm wondering if he would enjoy a roundup—an authentic roundup out in the more remote areas of the ranch. It would give him time to see what the ranch is really all about. He's taken to riding with ease and this is more than just riding a fence looking for a hole that donkeys escaped through. The boys love it. And I have a long weekend, and Rowdy mentioned to me that when he got home from his honeymoon, the cattle would have to be driven from the east pastures over to the west pastures. Only problem is it takes two days and requires camping out one night."

She sat straighter as he spoke and smiled,

excitement in her eyes. "Oh, Tucker, I think he would love that. It sounds so, so exciting."

He chuckled. "Well, it's a cattle drive. As a cowboy, I love the drive and never miss it if I can help it. There is just something about being on the trail like that that takes you back to the basics. We'd originally put this one off because Rowdy's gone, but we can do it without him. And we could have it set up to start tomorrow if you want."

"I think it's a great plan. Gordon talked about loving the cattle drive, too. I think I remember him saying there was a pass you had to take them through and a cabin with corrals that had been built back in the early days of the ranch."

"That's right. You could come, too. If you think you could take off."

"I'll see what I can do. I might be able to have someone cover for me for the afternoon, and Camy's already set to work on Saturday."

"Then I'll call Morgan and Dad, and see what I can set up."

She smiled; there was relief and anticipation in that smile. "I'll talk to Abe as soon as he wakes up and fill him in on everything you and I have set up. I'll let you know how it goes."

"We have a plan."

Her eyes melted his heart when she looked at him. "Yes, we do. And that's why I called you, because I knew you would help me think this through and come up with something good. Thank you."

She would never know how much those words meant to him.

Standing, and knowing he needed to put space between them before he messed up and pulled her into his arms, he took her hand and tugged her from the swing. "That means a lot to me. Now, how about you head on inside and get some rest. You're going to need it."

She took a step toward him, as if she were

going to come in for a hug—or to rest her head against his thundering heart. But she stopped suddenly.

"Thank you. See you tomorrow, Tucker McDermott."

He watched her go. Only after she was inside and the door firmly shut behind her did he leave.

He whistled all the way home.

And didn't sleep a wink for the rest of the night.

Chapter Fifteen

The morning had been a whirlwind. Suzie had actually slept after Tucker left. She'd set her alarm for 5:00 a.m. and by 6:00 a.m. she was dressed in roundup-appropriate attire—just in case Tucker was able to organize everything as discussed. She went into Abe's room, sat on the edge of his bed and gently shook his shoulder to get him to wake up. "Abe, honey, I need to talk to you before I head to the shop."

Groggily he opened his eyes. "Why?"

She needed them to be back on good terms. This was killing her. Leaning down she cupped his face in her hands and laid her cheek against his. "I love you, Abe. I love you so much." When she rose up, she could see a brief glimpse of her son behind the mask of indifference. It was her hope.

"Look, I know last night was hard on you. But I've been doing some thinking." She told him of her plan to move them into town—that he would go to school here and could be friends with the boys, but that they needed their own place. She said she was going to begin preparing the apartment so that the following week they could move in.

"For real?"

"Yes, and since our things are already stored there it shouldn't take too long to get it cleaned and painted. It's nothing fancy but it'll be ours."

He sat up, as if excited at the thought, which thrilled her. Then she told him what Tucker was doing, and asked him if he wanted to help with the roundup, if they had it. She worried briefly that he would say no.

"So, you're coming, too?"

She nodded. "Unless you'd rather I didn't. But when we get home, you can come into town with me and you and I will work on the apartment."

She was relieved to see excitement filter into his eyes. "Okay. Then that sounds good. I'd… Mom, I'd like you to go."

She very nearly started crying. Had that been part of the problem? He'd felt they were at a distance, too? "Then if you don't mind, let Tucker know that we're going if he gets it set up. He'll call me and I'll come straight here. I just need to get to town and line up someone to run the shop while I'm out." She'd been so blessed to have Camy, the teen was so reliable and she really enjoyed the shop. If only she could find someone to keep it open in the day at times like this, when she had to leave.

In the end, she found the most unlikely people to watch the shop and take orders for her—Chili and Drewbaker dropped by when she was about to start calling the handful of applicants.

"We're the perfect candidates for the job this morning," Chili said. "We're here right now, and you've got time to show us what to do before you hit the road to the ranch and hop on a horse."

"That's right. By the time you make a few calls and find one of them there applicants who could start at a minute's notice it could very well be noon, and then you'd have no time to show them anything. It could be a mess."

"A real mess," Chili agreed. "So, you can trust us two to watch the store for you, keep our hands off the flower arrangin' and take money for anything anyone wants to buy off the walls or counters. How does that sound?"

She laughed. "Y'all are really serious?"

"Sure we are," Drewbaker assured her. "You go spend time with your son and Tucker. And the rest of them kids at the ranch. You don't worry about a thing. We'll keep the doors open till Camy gets here and everything will be just fine."

She asked herself if she was just plain crazy. But no, these two sweethearts were competent men who, she was realizing, had hearts of gold.

"Then I accept your offer. I'll pay—"

"You'll do no such thing," Chili got out first, with Drewbaker saying something similar.

"We're doing this because we care and the good Lord saw fit to have us walk in here right when you needed us."

"Thank you, you two are sweethearts." She gave them each a hug then got busy showing them what they needed to know.

She'd run upstairs before opening that morning and had surveyed the apartment more thoroughly than she had the first day. She'd been intent then on staying at the ranch, but today she took in everything. It would work. With elbow grease and dust bunny attacking, she and Abe could be here by the following weekend. Abe could have a home of his own once more.

By noon she was heading back out to the ranch. Tucker had called as she was about to head out the door with a smile and a wave to Drewbaker and Chili.

"We're on," he said, his voice deep and excited against her ear. "We're having a roundup."

Suzie couldn't get to the ranch fast enough. This was about Abe, but in her heart of hearts she knew that something between her and Tucker had shifted. And the anticipation of exploring what and where that could lead had her pressing the gas pedal and driving hard for the ranch.

By midafternoon they were nearing the valley where the large herd waited for them. Tucker had explained that they were driving the small herd of cattle that was ahead of them from the pastures near the ranch house to join a larger herd over the rise. Then they would drive the two herds through the pass and over to fresh grazing lands. Then they would take the cattle in the pastures there and load them in cattle trailers bound for sale.

He explained some of the ins and outs of the cattle business as they rode beside each other, filling time, she knew, but it was interesting. She could tell that he loved the ranch and the ranching aspects of it.

"Can I ask you why, if you love this so much, you are sheriff instead of being more deeply involved in some aspect of the ranch? I know it's personal, and you don't have to tell me, but I'm curious."

"I hadn't planned on being a law enforcement officer. I'd planned on a career in the marines. But I got talked into running by my family. They knew it would help me to feel like I was making a difference. And it has. I needed that after what happened with Gordon."

She'd thought as much. "You're good with the boys, too. And you give back in that way."

He smiled at her, and her insides felt as if she'd just gone airborne over a speed bump.

"Thanks. I know I love this. And I'm glad you've come along."

"Thanks again for getting it together."

They reached the top of the hill. And below them was an enormous valley. Cattle were everywhere.

Tucker reined in his horse, and she did the same, bringing Cupcake to a standstill beside him.

"Wow. Unbelievable."

"Yeah, it's pretty awesome."

"It certainly is."

He pointed across the expanse to where Abe and the other teens were on the far edge of the cattle, riding back and forth, waving their ropes and moving the cattle forward. "Abe's holding his own. Look at him go after that stray that's running the wrong direction."

From this distance they couldn't see the boys' faces; she recognized individuals more from their mannerisms and body size. She had picked Abe out instantly. But so had Tucker. It touched her deeply that he was close enough to her son that he could do that from this distance.

"Oh, Tucker, he is having a blast."

"He's out there learning from some of the best. I'm glad we did this a week early, because it enabled Wes and Joseph to join in before they head back to Huntsville on Sunday. Wes is a cowboy of cowboys. He can't be outridden or out-roped. Abe is hanging close to him.

"You ready to ride down there and get involved?"

"I think so."

"Sure you are," he said with a wink. "I'm going to make a cowgirl out of you yet."

He laughed and nudged his horse into a

lope. Cupcake followed—and, ready or not, Suzie rode!

It was amazing as they rode down the hill toward the cattle. She felt free with the wind flowing across her skin. She was very grateful for the day she'd spent riding the fence on Cupcake looking for the donkey escape route. At least she didn't feel as though she was going to topple off the horse and land in the dirt.

Tucker had explained earlier that she was to crowd the cattle so that they would leave the grass they were eating and move along with the others. Once moving, it was fairly easy to keep them going, but every so often one would lag behind or break for freedom. That was when she would have to work with Cupcake to get between the heifer and wherever it was she was trying to escape to.

That was the tricky part.

But for now, she was quite proud of the fact that she was pushing the cattle along almost as if she'd been born to do this. Of course, there was no telling how many roundups ole Cupcake had been involved in. The truth was that Suzie could probably drop the reins, and the horse would have gone on doing exactly what it was doing.

Even so, Suzie felt exhilarated with the ride.

Dust and mooing, mingled with the usual whoops and hoots of the boys, was the music of the day over the range. The sun lifted high and hot in the Texas sky—fitting for such an adventure, Suzie decided, though the beads of perspiration and grime weren't the most endearing aspects of the day.

No, there was no getting around the fact that a roundup was a hot job.

But Suzie found herself smiling most of the way. Smiling so much that her teeth kept drying out and her lips kept getting stuck. Not exactly glamorous, but Suzie could see now there was a reason cowboys were cowboys. There was definitely something about the process that drew a certain type of person.

She was startled to find that she *was* that sort of person. Of course, when her backside started aching it dawned on her that she might not be able to move the next day. Suddenly a cow broke and ran straight toward her, jolting her out of her daydreaming. Cupcake instantly tried to jump in front of the renegade, and Suzie nearly fell out of the saddle. Grabbing the saddle horn, she regained her balance. Then, determined to do her job, she tugged on the reins, wheeled Cupcake around, and they loped after the calf. The old horse knew exactly what she was doing. They rounded in front of the cow and, to Suzie's pride, the animal turned back. "We did it!" she exclaimed, patting Cupcake's neck as they fell back into the lineup.

She caught Tucker smiling at her. She gave him a thumbs-up.

"You're a natural," he called.

"I love it!" Anticipation for the rest of the day filled her. Now Suzie knew exactly why the boys whooped and yelled "Yee-haw!"

The cattle were mooing and plodding along the streambed that went down the center of the ravine. It made for the perfect containment passage as they moved to the other side of the ranch.

"There's Nana," Suzie said, spying her in the valley.

Tucker grinned. She was cooking on her big barbecue pit, which she always pulled to the area behind her old truck. It was her version of a chuck wagon. "Nana married my grandfather and started driving her truck-wagon out to the roundups to feed the cowboys long before Dad had been born. It's a tradition."

"That's so wonderful. They must have been perfect for each other."

He looked at Suzie, she was so beautiful. "They were."

By the time they arrived, she had the sausage links hot and sizzling on the grill, and the tortillas warm and ready for a feast of sausage wraps followed by peach cobbler. The kids ate as if they hadn't seen food in a week, and even Suzie ate like a cowhand.

"How are you holding up?" he asked, moving to stand beside her.

She was standing real still as she ate, and he figured it might be because it hurt too bad to sit.

"Well, there are parts of my anatomy that I no longer feel, they've gone numb. And then there are other parts that are screaming in pain with every move I make."

He chuckled. "Thought that was why you were standing so stiffly."

"Yup. If I hadn't had such a great morning, I would kick you with my boot—but it would hurt too bad. And I have had the time of my life."

Her eyes were twinkling, and if he'd had a camera he'd have taken her picture.

"I'm sorry about the soreness. Riding does take some getting used to by greenhorns."

"Greenhorns! That's an understatement. And believe me, I have no idea how I'm going to climb back up into that saddle."

"Tucker will help you out," Nana called. "Don't you worry. I've got some great liniment I'll give you tonight that will help. Tucker, do you think the rain is going to hold off?"

He'd been studying the storm clouds and he could see his dad, Morgan and Chet, their top hand, over by the horses studying them, too. He wanted this experience to keep being positive. Rain added a whole different aspect to a roundup.

They especially didn't need the rain on the leg of the trip that was coming up. He could hear the river roaring up ahead as the stream turned and fed into the river that cut through Sunrise Ranch. The cattle would travel a short distance along the flowing river, but then an arm of the ravine would fork and the cattle would walk up an embankment and into the next section of the ranch.

The river flowed pretty good on a wet day, and since they'd had heavy rains up-river two days before, it would be rushing through this narrow, curved section and bottleneck farther downriver into some dangerous rapids.

Suzie was doing a good job riding beside nine-year-old Sammy at the moment. "Y'all stay on the left side of the cattle until we make it to the fork. You know the rules, Sammy," he called, and the kid gave him a nod. Sammy had learned to respect the river's power and Tucker knew he'd follow the rules.

Abe burst from the brush chasing a runaway heifer back into the herd. Then he pulled up beside them.

"That one gave me some trouble but I got

it. This is great." He grinned. Tucker hadn't seen a smile from the kid in over a week.

"You're making a top hand, that's for certain," Tucker assured him. "Just stay away from the embankment."

The river was growing louder.

"I'll be back." Tucker rode up ahead through the cattle and toward where his dad, Morgan and Chet were taking the outer positions beside the herd. Each would take the position at the opening as they came to it, waving the cattle off from the water and in the right direction. Then he'd move forward as the next man and his section moved through. Tucker was the last.

Behind him, he heard a shout and saw Abe take off after another runaway. Sammy went to help. Up front, the first of the cattle had reached the river. Everything was going well as the last cattle began feeding through. Tucker took Chet's place on the flat rock that was buffeted by the river as it raced past. Now he could see the water was higher than they'd realized and building small rapids, even this far upstream. He glanced back at Suzie just as she had Cupcake block a calf from making a run for it. The move took her to the very back of the herd, where there were no animals between her and the river.

He was about to yell for her to move up when the heifer Abe and Sammy had followed into the woods came blasting from the trees as if its tail was on fire. Cupcake jumped but held her ground. Suzie, in her excitement to cut the calf off, jabbed the horse too hard with the heels of her boots. Cupcake did what she was asked and bolted after the calf. Everything seemed to happen in slow motion as Suzie came too close to the rock edge. Tucker urged his horse just as the calf twisted around and bolted straight into Cupcake.

Tucker watched, helpless, as the poor horse danced sideways then reared when the frightened calf rammed it.

Eyes wide, Suzie tried to hold on as Cupcake pawed the air. Though the horse found its balance it was too late for Suzie as she pitched backward out of the saddle and into the river below.

Chapter Sixteen

Tucker yelled to draw everyone's attention as Suzie hit the water and went under, then reappeared flailing in the swift current. The current dragged her under almost instantly. Tucker was already reaching for his rope before she hit the water—his heart stopping but his mind reacting.

Urging his horse forward, he charged down the bank along the uneven edge of the river. Praying for Suzie to reappear again, he knew he was her best shot as she came up fighting downstream. "Yah!" he shouted, urging his horse to increase speed as he started his rope spinning above his head.

Suzie was fighting, but he had to get her before she rounded the curve. This throw mattered more than any other he'd ever made, he knew, as he sent the loop after her.

The rope sailed through the air—his prayers flying with it that God would direct its path.

It landed over her and she grasped it. Then he had his horse sit back on its heels and begin backing up, pulling her from the water.

"You got her," Sammy yelled.

When she was almost to shore, Tucker wrapped the rope around the horn and threw himself from the saddle. Letting one hand slip down the length of the line, he raced into the water, pulling her the rest of the way ashore.

His heart pounded as he hauled her from the water and into his arms. Terror gripped him, now that it was done, and he clung to her. She clutched him as he kissed the top of her head.

"You're okay now. You're safe," he said, caressing her hair, trying to soothe her nerves, unable to hold her tight enough.

"Thank you," she gasped. "I'm sorry. I shouldn't have put Cupcake in that position. You told me. I just got excited." She was rambling, looking up at him.

Tucker shook his head. "It's okay, Suzie. It wasn't your fault. You're safe, and that's all that matters."

He'd almost lost her before he'd had the opportunity to tell her he loved her.

"You saved me," she whispered, the sweetest expression on her face.

"I wasn't about to lose you. I love you, Suzie. I couldn't lose you." He kissed her long and hard, not caring who saw—not thinking about who was around. His only thought was he had the woman he loved in his arms and she was safe.

"Mom!" Abe yelled, racing up on his horse, bringing everything around them back into focus. Everyone was rallying around them.

"I'm okay. Tucker pulled me out," she said, though it was obvious what had happened. But Abe didn't seem interested in that. His face contorted in anger.

"You *kissed* him," he accused, his expression twisting with rage.

"Hey, son, hold on," Tucker said, stepping in.

"I'm not your son!" Abe exclaimed. Then he spun his horse and took off riding as fast as he could go.

"Abe," Suzie cried, her hand coming to her mouth.

"I'll get him." Anger, alarm and empathy forged together for the kid. Looking at the ashen expression on Suzie's face, he moved to his horse, swung into the saddle and went after Abe. "Take care of her," he called to his dad as he rode past.

"You need help?"

He shot his dad a look over his shoulder.

"No, we'll meet you at the cabin." And he buckled down low and rode like the wind.

Abe needed a showdown. And he wanted it with Tucker.

And Tucker understood it, and was prepared to take whatever the kid needed to throw at him.

But one thing the kid needed to know was that his mother didn't deserve what he'd just thrown at her.

The threatening rain clouds that had hovered over the day had darkened ominously and the wind had picked up. Tucker rode hard, following the path through the trees that Abe had taken.

A storm wouldn't be good for the roundup. They'd planned on camping at the cabin halfway to their destination. But would they make it before the storm hit? He glanced at the sky, then back at the trail. His dad would handle it.

He had to find Abe. He had to get to the root of this…finally.

When he topped the ridge he spotted the boy riding his horse across the open pasture at a crazy speed. The danger of the horse hitting a hole and breaking its leg, or falling and rolling on Abe, was high.

Yelling wouldn't do any good, since he suspected that even if Abe could hear him, he wouldn't listen.

Tucker prayed again that Abe would make it to the trees and be forced to slow down again. At the speed they were going, it didn't take long to cross the meadow.

Just as Tucker made it to the trees, the skies opened up with torrential rain. God answered prayers sometimes in mysterious ways. Abe would have to slow down now.

Ahead of him a lightning bolt lit the dark sky and thunder instantly shattered the silence with a deafening blast—reminding him of a mortar exploding.

It was too close.

"Abe!" he shouted, just as another bolt of lightning and crack of thunder split the sky open. Texas thunderstorms blew in with unexpected power some days, and this was not weather they'd anticipated when they'd chosen to bring the boys on this cattle drive. He heard a yell up ahead and plunged forward through the brush that tore at him. He pulled up short when he saw Abe, thrown from his horse, lying sprawled on his back. As soon as he saw Tucker, he tried to scramble up but couldn't. Within seconds Tucker was out of the saddle and kneeling beside him.

"Go away," Abe yelled, wiping rain and maybe tears from his face as he glared at Tucker.

Tucker ignored him, too intent on getting him to safety. "Are you hurt? We need to get out of this."

"I can get myself out of this. I don't need you. Stay away from my mother."

Lightning cracked and thunder rolled and the sound of a tree splintering could be heard somewhere not too far away.

"Where does it hurt?" Tucker demanded. His commanding tone, one developed and fine-tuned in war zones, left no room for denial. His unwavering gaze locked on to Abe's.

"My ankle," Abe snapped, giving in.

Tucker wasted no time. Slipping his arm under Abe's, he hauled the teen up. "Here we go, roles reversed from our first meeting."

Abe grunted, and grimaced with pain.

"I'm going to get us out of this weather before we get struck by lightning or hit by a falling tree. You can blast me with whatever you want once you're safe. Hang on."

Abe winced as Tucker hauled him up and over his shoulder. Intent on his mission to get the kid to safety, Tucker moved at a fast pace through the woods.

"Where are you going?" Abe asked, his hands pressing against Tucker's shoulder blades to balance himself.

"There's a cave near here where we can

sit out the storm. Rowdy discovered it when we were kids. You were heading right to it and didn't know it." Tucker didn't say it out loud, but he looked at that coincidence as divine intervention. He'd put them not fifty yards from the cave.

In the woods, it was almost as dark as night with the storm clouds blotting out the sun above the canopy of trees. But even still, he knew where the cave was. "Me and my brothers spent many a night in this cave we're going to. Rowdy discovered it after our mother died. It became our shelter when the grief overwhelmed one of us."

Abe didn't say anything, but Tucker felt him tense. The cave came into view, a ledge more than an actual cave, it would provide shelter from the storm.

Ducking low he carried Abe to the farthest corner from the opening and set him down gently so that he could lean back against the rock wall.

Abe wiped water from his face, his gaze

dug into Tucker as he pushed the leg of Abe's jeans up and then began to ease off his boot. "Your ankle is swollen, all right. We'll need to elevate it."

"You kissed my mother." The words were accusing.

Tucker had lost his head after pulling Suzie from the water. He shouldn't have kissed her like that in front of Abe and the others. But he'd lost his head…he hadn't been thinking.

"Yeah, I did." The truth was all he could do. "Abe, talk to me," he urged. When Abe said nothing, Tucker moved over to a thick, flat rock that was about a foot wide and he pushed it to the side, exposing a hole where a baggie of matches and lighters were stored.

He held them up for Abe to see. "These have been here for a long time. And the wood, too. We had a rule growing up—anyone could come here when they needed to get away, but they had to leave wood and matches for the next person's first fire." He opened the bag and pulled out the box of matches. "It's a good idea, even all these years later."

Abe had crossed his arms and pressed his back into the rock as if to get as far away from Tucker as he could.

Tucker studied the wood and the matches. "This isn't left over from me fifteen years ago. I think someone else has been visiting here since me and my brothers and your dad were here."

"My dad came here?" he asked gruffly.

"Yeah, he had times when he needed to be alone, too. When your family dies or cuts you loose in the world before your time… it leaves a lot of anger. You aren't the only one who's ever dealt with them, you know. Your dad needed quiet time to think, too. So did I and my brothers. So do most of the boys who come to Sunrise Ranch. And no, you aren't like them. You had two parents who loved you deeply and cared deeply for you. You still have your mom."

Abe looked sullen.

"Being here among these boys doesn't mean you're like them. I know you are having abandonment issues, but there is no reason to, because you haven't been and never were. You need to let that go."

Abe glared at him then looked away, studying the rain pouring over the edge of the entrance like a waterfall blocking out the world. "Yeah, Wes has been talking to me."

Leave it to Wes. The kid might be determined to be a champion bull rider, but his calling was as a counselor.

"That's good. You need to talk to others. Wes is a great one to talk to."

"He told me I need to let it go. I tried. That shrink said the same thing. But…"

"You don't want anyone messing with your mom."

He nodded.

Tucker fought off a sigh that wanted freedom. What could he say? He wasn't about to make promises to the kid he couldn't keep. "I had planned on bringing you here, but things kept getting in the way," he said instead. "I think today God said it was time."

Grabbing a handful of kindling he started working on a fire. Within moments, a small but warm fire glowed between them. Abe had grown more sullen and glared at the fire, lost in his own world of hurt and anger.

After a few quiet moments he rubbed his ankle. "Because of you, my dad is dead."

The words stretched between them like dead weight. "I would have given my life for your dad. But, instead, your dad gave his life for—not just me, but his entire unit. I hate that he died, but, Abe, he would have done it for any one of the guys in the unit. This wasn't about me, at all, but about the kind of man your dad was. I hate it with all my heart that it killed him. But he was a proud marine and his own man. He chose to lay his life down for me and the others."

Abe was so tense that he looked as though he might break in half. His eyes misted. "He left me. Left Mom."

Tucker's heart hurt for Abe. He remembered well the feeling of abandonment he and his brothers felt when their mother died. "He didn't abandon you, Abe. He made the choice he could live with."

Abe glared at him. "But he didn't live."

The truth played across Tucker's thoughts as clear as springwater. "If your father hadn't at least tried to save me—if he hadn't tried to stop the shooter—it wouldn't have been something he could have lived with. Your dad was a man who followed a code of ethics. He would never have walked away from a fellow marine in need without first doing what he needed to do. Even if that meant dying."

Big tears streamed down Abe's face, built-up pain and grief escaping in a river of release. Tucker looked at the small fire and prayed that this could be God's time of healing for this kid. Reaching out, he laid his hand on Abe's shoulder. "You are a strong young man, Abe. You are, after all, your father's child and your mom's."

Abe brushed his damp cheeks with the backs of his hands, and nodded.

Encouraged, Tucker continued, "You are made of tough stuff. The anger you've locked inside is normal. No one wants to lose someone they love. Someone they need. Me and my brothers have walked through this valley, too—and, in many ways, your dad and all of these boys here at Sunrise Ranch. You are not alone."

"I know," he whispered.

"But, Abe, your grief and the pain you feel is uniquely yours, and you have to grieve in your own way. The same goes for your mother."

Abe swallowed hard and stared at him.

"Eventually, you will both have to move

forward. To be healthy, it's the only way. Your mother is trying."

Abe remained silent and Tucker prayed his words were sinking in to Abe's heart.

"And that goes for me, too. Your dad's death is similar to Jesus giving His life for all of us so that we could live. It was a gift beyond measure. And I'm unworthy of it but struggling to be a man of honor and strength who Gordon would be proud of. And I'll always be here for you. And for your mother."

Abe studied him.

"Why did you kiss my mother?"

He held Abe's gaze and thought carefully about how best to answer him. "Because I've come to care deeply for your mother. Today, it terrified me when I thought I'd lost her. I kissed her out of relief." It was the truth, part of it anyway. Now was not the time to tell Abe that he loved Suzie.

The flames flickered in the kid's eyes, exposing so much pain. He nodded. "Good. I like you, Tucker, but…"

"It's okay, Abe. You don't have to explain. We'll get through this."

Chapter Seventeen

"They'll be all right," Randolph said, coming to stand beside Suzie at the window of the camp house, where they were escaping the storm. It had been built by Randolph's dad when he'd bought the ranch. "Tucker will find him, and they'll find shelter and sit this storm out."

Chilled to the bone, and not because of the weather, she wrapped her arms around her waist and took a deep breath. "I hope so."

"I know my son and he's resourceful. Plus, he and his brothers have roamed every inch of this ranch and know places to hole up that even I don't know. As soon as this passes over, I'll send all my ranch hands out to search, too, so don't worry. Tucker will know that. As soon as it's safe to travel he'll be on the move."

"If he can. If they're both able," she added.

"Yes. Now, would you want to come help scrounge something up to feed these boys? You don't have to help but it would give you something to do other than stand here and worry."

Morgan and Chet had immediately started a fire when they'd made it inside the cabin, and all the boys were gathered around it to warm themselves after being drenched. Wes was once more entertaining them with stories of his first semester of college and bull-riding escapades.

"Yes, I'll do that. I know they are not going to materialize outside this window in between lightning bolts."

She followed him to the corner where the rustic kitchen area had been set up. There was a gas stove and cabinets where she found large and small containers of canned food. There were several gallon-size cans of chili and they opted for that. There was also a large glass jar with a label on it that said Nana's Cocoa.

"As you can tell, Nana keeps the place stocked up for emergencies, large or small."

Suzie smiled up at Randolph. "I have a feeling she stays on top of any and every situation that could arise."

He smiled the devastating smile that he'd passed down to each of his sons. "My mother is a wonder, that is for certain."

Working as a team they prepared the meal while Chet and Morgan donned slickers from a closet and went out to check on the horses and the livestock.

Time ticked by, and Suzie tried not to think about it. Still, Abe's fury at seeing Tucker kissing her kept flashing through her mind. When she'd been in the river, the undercurrent was so strong, and though she'd been fighting, she'd felt like a rag doll at its mercy. When Tucker had pulled her out of that water and wrapped her in his arms she'd known she never wanted to leave the security and love she felt there.

Love. It had become so clear that she'd fallen for the lawman despite all the reasons not to. Despite the fact that she'd had no desire to fall for anyone, and especially him.

But she had.

Still, Abe's angry outburst had instantly brought her back to the real world. She pushed the turmoil in her mind away and concentrated on boiling water for hot chocolate and stirring the large pot of chili.

When the food was almost ready, Randolph asked her if she could handle it alone, and when she said yes he thanked her, then grabbed a slicker and went out to find Morgan and Chet.

She couldn't help but wonder if he was more concerned than he was letting on.

Randolph had found a stash of paper cups

and bowls—bless Nana's heart—and he'd placed them on the rough counter separating the kitchen from the living area where the boys were. Shutting her mind off, she focused on her task.

"Time to eat, boys," she called, and that was all it took to start a stampede.

"Thanks, Ms. Suzie," Sammy said, and more thanks raced from the others as they came through the line and she ladled chili into their bowls.

"You think Tucker and Abe are okay?" B.J. asked.

"Yes, they are," Wes answered from behind the little boy. Wes met her gaze with solid eyes. Eyes that said he believed what he was saying. "Tucker will make sure of it."

He smiled, and Joseph agreed instantly, and through the trepidation that was suffocating her, she smiled back at them. She had fallen in love with all of these boys in the weeks since she and Abe had been here, and in the short time Wes and Joseph had been home she'd done the same with them.

"I believe they are all right," she said, realizing that in her heart of hearts she knew that Tucker would not have stopped until he found Abe. The surety of that wrapped around her reassuringly.

The problem was, had he found Abe yet? After the boys all had their food, she walked to the window and stared out into the storm.

"Please let them be safe, dear Lord. Please," she whispered the words of prayer and worked at forcing herself to believe that God would bring Abe home to her. She couldn't lose someone else…didn't want to think about it.

God hadn't brought Gordon home to them, so she knew there were no guarantees in this life.

The rain was hitting the window sideways, the wind was blowing so hard, and rivers of it ran down the pane making it almost impossible to see anything but a blurry gray evening turning into night.

Lightning sizzled across the sky, and right on its heels another bolt made a jagged stab at the earth so close that she jumped.

Closing her eyes, she prayed harder and fought the helplessness that engulfed her.

Abe had run away because of her. He saw Tucker kissing her, and—if she admitted the truth—he saw her kissing Tucker back.

She'd been trying all evening to deny it, but she couldn't. She had to take the blame and not put it solely on Tucker. She'd known in the water, when she'd believed she could be about to die, that she'd regretted not giving the emotions she felt for Tucker a fighting chance.

And what were these emotions?

She'd fallen in love with the strong, caring cowboy. But what if Abe couldn't accept that?

What then?

* * *

The storm had settled in for most of the night, so Tucker and Abe had sat it out inside the dank but dry shelter. He'd worried all night about Suzie and prayed that she knew he had her son safe. Abe had finally fallen to sleep after their conversation. And, somewhere along the way, Tucker had slept for a short while. But the sun wasn't quite up when he shook Abe awake.

"It's cleared up. I think we should get started. Dad and Morgan will have the ranch swarming with folks searching for us if we don't get back soon after sunrise. Plus, your mom is probably sick with worry and no sleep."

He looked ashamed. "I'm sorry for that."

"She'll just be glad you're okay."

"I'm going to try and take care of her."

Tucker gave the boy a nod. "You'll do a fine job of it."

Abe had told him the same thing Suzie had, that they were moving into the apartment. It was probably for the best, and time would make things better. "Where are the horses?"

"They're either near or will have headed back toward the ranch. If they've made it back before us, then that will make everyone worry all the more. So we better get going."

"Okay."

Tucker had already put out the fire. He helped Abe stand, drew Abe's arm over his shoulder, and they started down the hill, moving as fast as they could, given the sprained ankle.

The sun began to peek over the horizon quickly; a good thing, since the ground was slippery.

They worked their way down the hillside they'd ridden up. They didn't talk much, but Abe didn't seem as sullen or angry. When they made it to the bottom of the hill and were on more even land, traveling across an open pasture, Tucker asked how Abe was.

The kid hefted a shoulder. "Fine, I guess. I thought about what you said, and I know my dad would want better of me. For my mom. I'm the man of the house now."

"Yes, that's true. But you don't need to let that pressure you."

Abe gave him a long look as they trudged forward. "I'm going to try and use it like you're doing. I'm going to try and let my dad's death make me a better man. Not that you weren't a good man. I know all about the men you saved and how you are a hero. The guys talk about it all the time. Wes showed me stuff on the internet. Said you didn't put any of your medals out for display. So I'm not saying that. I'm just saying, you know, you're…you're trying to carry my dad's torch along with you."

Emotion clogged Tucker's throat. He nodded.

Abe gave a sad smile. They were halfway across the pasture when Morgan and

Chet emerged from the woods leading their horses.

Tucker hadn't ever been so glad to see his brother and his friend. With their help they'd get back to Suzie sooner.

And she and her son would finally have the fresh start she'd been praying for.

And he would hang in the background and give them room.

The sun was barely up, but everyone was saddled and ready to ride. Tucker's dad hadn't slept all night, either. Neither had Morgan and Chet, who'd headed out as soon as the lightning had eased up and the rain had turned to a drizzle. To ease the wait, they'd told stories of life on the ranch, and as worried as she was, Suzie had found herself laughing at the antics of the kids. With all of the activities that went on, there was never a shortage of stories. But now, she was ready to find Abe. And Tucker.

She was about to climb into the saddle when she heard one of the boys yell.

"They're coming!"

Suzie spun around to see Tucker and Abe riding from the woods with Morgan and Chet.

Relief and love raced through her in a riot of happy emotion.

Rushing forward, she met Abe as he eased from his saddle, hopped on one foot and wrapped his arms around her.

"I'm sorry, Mom," he said, hugging her as tightly as she hugged him. It was the first real hug she'd had from him in months. Her knees almost buckled from the shock and joy of it.

With her heart full to overflowing, she held him close and met Tucker's eyes. "Thank you," she mouthed silently, and then to her son she said, "Don't worry about any of that, Abe. I love you and am so glad you are okay."

"And you, too, Mom. I didn't even tell

you I was glad you were safe after Tucker pulled you from the river."

She assured him she'd known he was, despite what had transpired afterward.

The boys had held back, giving them time for their reunion, but now they rushed forward and encircled them, welcoming Abe and asking what had happened.

She wanted to know as much as they did. It was obvious something had happened to his ankle but he seemed okay. Giving him a last squeeze around the waist, she backed away and let him talk to his friends.

"Tucker caught up to me after the storm hit. It was bad, I sprained my ankle, too. But he knew of a cave and we made it there and spent the night."

"Sweet!" Wes said. "That's *my* cave. It's a good thinkin' place."

"Yeah, that's for sure," Abe agreed. "But me and Tucker mostly talked and watched the fire while the rain and the lightning went crazy. What'd y'all do?"

"We had chili," B.J. exclaimed. "And it was *good, good, gooood!*"

Tucker moved to stand beside her, keeping a distance between them that was obvious.

"Thank you for bringing him back to me." She wanted to reach out and touch him, but she didn't. He was holding himself at a distance, anyway—could she blame him? *No.*

"I think Abe is going to be all right. Talk to him, I believe he may have turned a corner toward healing."

"I'll do that. Are you all right?"

"Don't worry about me." He didn't wait for her to reply. Instead, he went back to his horse and stepped into the stirrup, threw his leg over the saddle and looked down at the boys. "Okay, boys, we started this job and we're going to finish it. We've got cattle to round up."

That was all it took for the boys to head to their horses. Abe was grinning as he limped to his.

"Abe, you need to have that ankle looked at," Tucker warned.

"It's better. Sitting in a saddle's not going to hurt it," he said, using his good foot to saddle up. "Let's roll," he said, looking every bit the born-and-bred cowboy.

Suzie was so proud of him.

They'd talk later.

There were some important issues that had to be discussed.

"Come on, Ms. Suzie, it's roundup time. Ain't you comin'?" B.J. called, riding over to her. She had to smile at the little boy.

"B.J., I wouldn't miss it for the world. Goodness, you look like you grew a foot last night. I was looking down at you and now I'm looking up. What happened?"

He giggled. "I got on my horse."

"Oh, is that what you did? Well, hang on and I'll get on mine, and we can round them up together, how's that?"

He grinned. "Awesome!"

She caught Abe smiling at her from his

horse, and it felt as though the sun had just come out after the terrible storm.

What, she wondered, had gone on between Tucker and Abe out there in the midst of that storm?

Whatever it was, it was an answer to her prayers, and she couldn't wait until there was a private moment where she and Tucker could talk.

About a lot of things.

Chapter Eighteen

Edwina hustled from the Spotted Cow's kitchen, plopped two plates of food in front of a pair of cowboys in the corner, then headed Tucker's way. The sharp-witted waitress took one look at him, poked her pencil behind her ear and grimaced. "Sheriff, you look like roadkill—awful handsome roadkill, but *awful* bein' the key word here. What happened to you?" She held up her hands. "No, wait. You need some strong coffee first, and then you can explain why you have marched in here and completely wrecked my belief that you always look magazine-perfect."

He wasn't going to argue—he needed strong coffee and some of Ms. Jo's coconut pie. And he was proud to see that he didn't even have to ask for it. After loading up the horses in the trailers that the hands had waiting for them at the end of the roundup, Tucker had watched all of the boys and Abe pile into trucks and head back to the ranch.

There had been no time for a private talk with Suzie. He'd just been able to ask if she was all right after her fall in the river. Since there hadn't been much time before he'd gone after Abe, he had simply needed to make sure she was okay. She'd kept her distance. He'd longed to wrap his arms around her, but he didn't want to upset Abe or Suzie. Had she just reacted to his kiss earlier because she'd been terrified?

That question had been eating at him.

Edwina left him at the table and returned with a pot of coffee in one hand and a double portion of pie in the other. "Here," she said, plopping the pie in front of him then carefully filling his cup full of dark coffee. "You need sugar, so eat up. And then tell me what has happened to you."

The coffee burned a trail down his throat and the sweet, creamy pie acted like an IV of glucose as it rushed into his bloodstream. He'd taken a swig of the coffee and downed a forkful of pie before he realized Edwina was still watching him, her arms crossed and the half-full pot of coffee dangling from one hand.

Ms. Jo finished her conversation at a nearby table and came over to stand beside Edwina. Her bright eyes behind her round-rimmed glasses pierced deep as she, too, studied him.

"Somethin's up, Ms. Jo," Edwina drawled, cocking her head toward him. "Tucker's inhalin' your pie like you don't have fifteen more back there he can have if he really wanted them."

"And he looks worn out, to boot. Take care of the customers, Ed. I've got this."

"Sure thing, boss. You just give me the nod on whatever you need. And fill me in later."

Tucker took another bite of pie. Why not? The two of them obviously didn't need him in the conversation they were indulging in at his expense. And he needed the pie, the comfort and the sugar it provided.

Ms. Jo slid into the booth across from him. "That's your mama's recipe, and anytime you're feeling low, you eat that pie like a man dying of thirst."

He swallowed, savoring the pie, remembering how his mother used to make this for him whenever he asked. He took another swig of coffee. "I guess even a grown man needs a little reminder sometimes of the way things used to be."

Ms. Jo laid her hand over his and squeezed. "We all do. What's got you looking so down? I noticed at the wedding the other night that you looked distracted." She dipped her chin, and peeked at him over the rim of her glasses. "I kind of suspected it had a little something to do with Suzie."

Was he that easy to read? He never had been before. As a marine he'd needed to sometimes live behind a shield, but maybe there wasn't any way to hide an emotion as strong as love.

"You see too much, for a little short woman."

One brow hiked. "This little short woman has eyes just like everyone else. Believe me, it wasn't just me who saw you only had eyes for our newest resident. Her business is doing good. Except yesterday she put Drewbaker and Chili in charge of the cash register, so I'm thinking she might have a screw or two loose upstairs." She chuckled. "They had customers backed out the door, it was so full."

He laughed. "Yeah, she was in a bad way and needed to go on the roundup with us. Those two volunteered and she felt spending time with Abe was worth it."

"And with you, maybe?"

He sighed. "Maybe, but it's complicated."

"Love always is."

He dug his fork into the last bite of pie, not willing to admit that to anyone yet. "Ms. Jo, that was wonderful. Can I ask you something?"

"Anything."

"You remember how I was after mom died?"

She looked sad and thoughtful. "Yep. You looked like you carried the weight of the world on your shoulders. It took a long time for you to accept that she was gone and not coming back. You remember that, don't you?"

He toyed with his coffee. "Some of it. A lot of those first months are fuzzy for me."

"Grief does things like that. Why do you ask?"

"Abe, he's better. But I'm not sure he's ever going to completely get over his dad's death."

Ms. Jo shook her head. "Death makes a

mark on a soul. But love is patient and kind and perseveres. It never gives up. Do you know what I'm saying? I know whatever is going on between you, Suzie and Abe is complicated. But God can work even complicated out according to His plan. And His plan is always perfect."

If he loved Suzie, he'd have to be patient. And if he loved her, he'd have to be willing to accept what was best for her...even if that meant he wouldn't be in her life.

"Tucker, I know you've had a lot on your plate since returning home. Gordon's death was hard on this entire community. We loved that young man. And for him to give his life for his country—and for you—it just has been hard. But we see that pain that runs through you as you take care of all of our safety, protecting us in our little world. You need to find happiness like your brothers have. And my instincts tell me Suzie means more to you than you want to admit."

Oh, he knew exactly how much she meant to him. It just wasn't that simple. He downed another long draw of coffee and glanced toward the exit, looking for an escape route.

Ms. Jo's knowing smile unfurled. "That's what I thought. Sometimes God's plan for our lives comes from the worst of circumstances. Beauty from ashes, the Bible says."

"And some things are never meant to be."

Her eyes flashed. "You ever see a flower growing out of a tiny crack in the cement or a sliver of dirt in a rock face? It's against all odds that that beauty would rise up out of that hard, unforgiving rock, but it does. It fights the odds and flourishes. If God's in this, then you fight for it. Don't give up on it before it's even had time to root."

He'd come for the pie, but also this. Ms. Jo's encouragement always cut to the quick of the matter. But this time he just wasn't sure if fighting for what he wanted was the right thing to do.

* * *

By Wednesday, Suzie and Abe were moved into the apartment over the shop. Everyone at the ranch had acted as if they were moving to Alaska. It was touching, really, and she hoped it made Abe feel good that everyone was sad to see him move from the ranch property. Suzie had been so relieved when Nana and Randolph assured her they understood.

The place still needed painting, but by the time she'd cleaned, thrown out all the stored junk, laid carpets on the floors, placed photos and paintings on the walls, arranged her furniture with help from Tony, Abe and Caleb. And Jake had helped, too. Now the apartment had a homey feel to it and a coziness that helped her feel relaxed. There was nothing like a place of your own to call home. No matter how much she had enjoyed Nana's hospitality, it hadn't been home. No wonder Abe had felt a little displaced. Now they were surrounded by familiar things, *their* things, family items that spoke to their hearts.

They'd also made huge steps toward healing in the past week. And they were building on that.

She'd taken Abe to school then picked him up after work all week and they'd come home together. She'd fixed them supper, and they'd eaten together at the kitchen table that they'd owned since Abe was a baby. There was familiarity in their days. And Abe seemed content.

Everything was almost perfect, as though life was actually going to be good again. Except Suzie realized very quickly that she missed Tucker.

She hadn't seen him since the day he'd returned Abe to her. He hadn't stopped by the shop, and she hadn't been at the ranch as much, so she hadn't seen him there.

She thought a few times about going to his office, but she hadn't.

"Mom," Abe said on Friday evening, as

they drove home from seeing Dr. Livingston. "Are you happy?"

"Yes," she said, glancing at him. "Is something wrong? I thought you said everything was better. And you said that you talked to Dr. Livingston and it helped."

His eyes were deeply serious. "I'm doing good, Mom. I asked about you. The doc, she asked me how I thought you were doing, and I told her good. She asked me if you were seeing anyone, if you'd moved forward, and how I would feel about that."

Suzie's pulse jerked and she automatically pressed the brake. They were on the outskirts of town and she slowed as she glanced at him. "What did you tell her?"

He frowned. "I told her you were fine. That you were happy."

"I am." Tucker's smile filled her mind, she missed him so.

"Are you sure?" Glancing at him again, she realized he looked worried.

"What's the matter, Abe?"

"Nothing," he said, and stared out the window.

She wasn't sure what to make of his questions. She knew in her heart that she'd fallen in love with Tucker McDermott. It had happened watching him care for her son's welfare and try so hard to make up for the loss of Gordon. She just didn't know what to do about it.

She didn't know how Abe would feel about it. And suddenly he was asking these questions.

"I'm a young woman, though, Abe. I probably will remarry one day. But I don't want you to worry about that now. I want you to be comfortable with it. My main concern right now is that you grow and adjust to our life as it is now. I don't want you to worry about anything. Okay?"

"Okay, and, Mom, I'm okay. You can stop worrying about me. I promise."

Her heart swelled and thankfulness filled her to the brim. *Thank You, Lord.* She smiled.

Her GED test was in four weeks. She and Jolie had come up with a study plan that worked for her. She was reminded every time she sat down with her books that she might have never thought to do this until Tucker had suggested it to her.

He'd been so encouraging in all aspects of her move here and in her life going forward. And now he'd helped Abe profoundly. The night after they'd stayed in the cave together, Abe told her that Tucker had talked to him about the anger that he'd felt when he lost his mother when he was around Abe's age.

What touched her was that Abe had said he was trying to live a life that would make his dad proud.

There was no better tribute than that. And Tucker was responsible for this turnaround.

Suzie couldn't get him off her mind, and she wondered why he hadn't come by to see them. He'd just seemed to disappear after the roundup.

Of course, she knew he was down the street at the office, but…she knew he knew she'd moved into the apartment in town. If he wanted to see her, wouldn't he come by?

On Saturday morning she woke early. She had decided she needed to talk to Tucker, but first she had to work on flowers for a small wedding. She was unlocking the front of her shop when Tucker passed by in his SUV.

Her heart began pounding at just seeing him. She waved and he pulled into an empty parking space. His elbow rested in the open window. "Morning, ma'am. You're out bright and early."

He was so handsome, she could hardly breathe looking at him. Her fingers itched to cup his rugged jaw, and she realized how much she wanted to feel his arms around her and his lips on hers.

She'd been concentrating on Abe all week, but now… "I have a wedding today. They need the flowers before lunch, so I wanted to make certain they were done. You're out and about early, too."

"Yeah, I need some bodies to fill up the jail cells so I thought I'd get an early start. Have them full by noon."

She laughed, and his eyes twinkled.

"It sounds like we'll both be finished by lunch," he said.

She took a step toward him, moving to the edge of the sidewalk. "I—I've missed you, Tucker. I was hoping to talk to you."

He looked away, studying some distant point at the end of the street. "I've been busy."

"Oh, sure, I see."

"How's Abe? Jolie told me he's been participating in school all week. And Pepper told me that he's been coming in and cleaning stalls, even though his two weeks of duty ended on Thursday."

"He's doing great, Tucker. And yes, I've had to bring him home from the ranch the last two days with the windows down because he's been cleaning stalls. But he said he was helping the younger boys out with their chores."

Tucker smiled. "He's a good kid, Suzie. He's going to be all right."

She took a deep breath. "Yes, he is. Thanks to you."

Tucker studied her and the distance between them seemed like a chasm. "How are you?"

"I'm good. I—" She ached to touch him. But he hadn't moved, was just sitting there with the closed truck door between them. "I'm good. We're getting settled in and things are more normal now, with our things around us. I'm going to have to paint." She smiled at the thought of the day he'd come by when she was painting. "But no red."

He chuckled. "I won't complain."

"I've started studying for my GED and I've signed up for online classes for the fall semester."

"That's wonderful," he said, pride in his eyes that brought sudden tears to hers. "What's wrong?" he asked, alarmed.

She sniffed, and swiped at her eyes. "Oh, nothing. I— Oh, Tucker, I owe you so much."

He was out of the truck before she could blink. He swiped the tear from her cheek before she could do away with it. "Don't cry, Suzie. I don't want you to cry anymore. You don't owe me anything. You don't."

The intensity of his words startled her. "But I do," she said, meaning it with all of her soul.

"Everyone loved Gordon, and they, we, love you and Abe," he said. "I want you and Abe to be happy and healthy. I want you to move on with your life, not feel like you owe me. No more tears about that."

He stepped closer and the spicy scent of his aftershave, masculine and woodsy, wrapped around her. It was everything she could do not to step close and lay her head on his shoulder.

But he wasn't reaching for her. His arms remained at his sides.

"I do, and I always will," she said, firmly.

His brows dipped over frustrated eyes. "I've got to go to work. What's Abe doing today?" he asked, before he turned to go.

Frustrated by the conversation, she hid her feelings.

"I think he said Tony and Jake were going to pick him up and they were going to practice for the rodeo or something. He seemed excited about it."

"Yeah, I think they are holding some sort of exhibition this afternoon. You should come."

"I will."

He tipped his hat. "Good. See you there."

And he was gone. She watched him drive off and felt as if he'd erected an invisible wall between them.

She didn't like it.

They'd come through so much together.

Why, she wondered, did it seem as if he

was holding her at arm's length? Why had he not come around to check on them since the roundup?

She'd missed him, but she'd been so busy getting Abe settled that she hadn't let herself dwell on why he was missing from their lives. Instead of going into the shop, Suzie headed back up the stairs. She walked into Abe's room, suddenly knowing that, as wonderful as things had been in the past week, she needed to ask him a question.

Laughter and excitement filled the air inside the arena. Along with dust churned up from the donkeys as the boys ran around trying to herd them into a holding pen. Tucker leaned against the rails with Morgan and Rowdy, waiting to watch the boys rope calves as soon as the donkeys were moved out of the way. The boys huddled up suddenly and then little B.J. broke from the group and came barreling across the arena, his face red with enthusiasm.

"We're gonna ride us some donkeys!" he exclaimed.

"Donkeys?" Tucker asked, glancing at his brothers. They looked as surprised as he was. He'd told the boys that they were going to load them up later and take them back to Chili's, since the fence had been fixed earlier that week. As it turned out, Chili and Drewbaker had saddled up and found the broken fence and fixed it. They hadn't let him hear the end of it, either.

The other boys walked up, expectant looks on their faces. "Y'all planning on riding the donkeys?" he asked.

Tony stepped out of the group. "Well, sir, Chili told us we could. So we were hoping to do it before we take them away."

"We thought we'd give it a go," Abe added, grinning.

Tucker chuckled, liking the grin on Abe's face.

Morgan crossed his arms and studied them. "You boys think you're up to that?"

Highly insulted expressions instantly swept over the group, and a round of indignant "Yes, sirs" rolled between them.

"Then go for it," Morgan said. It was his call since he and Randolph were in charge of the foster program. "And good luck."

"Yeah, watch those back legs," Tucker warned over the eruption of excited whoops. "They aren't as mild as they look." He should know, remembering the lick his hip had taken.

He glanced toward the house, where Suzie was visiting with Nana, Lucy and Jolie. He'd seen her drive up a few minutes ago and had to fight himself hard to stay away. It had been a fight all week. And that morning, he'd very nearly broken his vow to himself and enveloped her in his arms when she'd gotten emotional thanking him. Talking about owing him.

But that was it. He didn't want her to owe him. He wanted her to love him. And he wanted Abe to be okay with that. Wanted Abe to love him, in fact.

The shouts and laughter of the boys drew the women's attention and they started toward the arena, probably realizing the roping was about to start.

"Hi," she said, to him and his brothers as she walked up. "The boys seem really excited about the roping."

Rowdy chuckled. "They're excited, all right. But it's not about roping."

"They're about to have a riding exhibition," Morgan said, winking at Jolie. "Y'all need to grab seats in the stands and get ready for a show. And we better get out there to make sure it doesn't get too rank and rowdy."

"What are they going to ride?" Suzie asked, pinning Tucker with curious eyes.

"We're about to have a little exhibition rodeo. The boys are going to *attempt* to ride the donkeys."

All the women's eyes widened in alarm.

"Won't they kick?" Suzie asked first.

"And buck, too?" Lucy added. "I'm just glad I'm not getting roped into this one. You have to watch these fellas, Suzie. The little sneaks will trick you into doing things you wouldn't normally do."

"B-but—" Suzie stammered, glaring at him. "It's too dangerous. Remember how they charged me?"

"Now, Suzie, boys will be boys. We'll be there watching out for them," he said, and knew that he planned to join in the fun… while watching for flying body parts. Anything would be safer today than spending time standing too close to Suzie.

He turned and headed toward the gate. Putting distance between them. It was getting harder and harder to stay away from her.

"You aren't serious?" Suzie called, startled that Tucker would walk away from her, as if she would be okay with this.

Suzie planted her hands on her hips as her words brought Tucker to a halt in his tracks. He turned—looking shocked that she would ask such a thing.

"Are you seriously about to let these boys ride those...those donkeys? You and I both know that they seem docile but are far from it. Look what that one did to you."

"Now, Suzie, don't get all bent out of shape—"

Her mouth dropped open. "'Bent out of shape,'" she huffed. "I saw firsthand what those measly animals can do. One kicked your legs right out from under you. And then, one charged me—tried to run me over and trample me!"

"Look, yes, there are a few dangers, but these boys know how to watch out for them. I just got a little too close the other day, is all."

"And that is supposed to make me feel better."

"I guess it doesn't, but this is cowboy

country. This is what we do for fun. You just need to relax. It's going to be all right. And, despite what you are thinking, it's going to be great for Abe."

He turned and continued on his way as if she'd never said anything. "Going to be fine, indeed," she mumbled, almost going after him.

"Suzie, come sit with me," Nana said, drawing her attention.

"I can't believe this," Suzie said, moving toward Nana.

"This is a ranch," Jolie said, coming up beside her. "They love doing things like this. It'll be fun. Rowdy and the others will minimize the risk, but honestly, kids get hurt falling off their bicycles. It'll be all right. You can't put kids in a bubble. They have to have some freedom. I think this is especially good for Abe. He needs to know he's tougher than he thinks." This coming from a champion kayaker—daredevil—had Suzie wondering if she was too overprotective.

Feeling as if she would explode with anxiety, Suzie forced a nod. She couldn't always protect Abe from everything. She just couldn't. And the truth was that she trusted Tucker and his family. She did have to let go some. She'd smother Abe if she didn't.

But could she relax enough to watch Abe ride?

The boys were having a blast. The donkeys were giving them the time of their lives and testing their abilities. Tucker wanted to enjoy the event but all he could think about was Suzie.

Abe came bouncing by, laughing even though he was clinging to a wild donkey's neck in his effort not to be thrown to the ground.

Tucker's gaze flew instantly to Suzie. To his surprise she was laughing. Her eyes were alive, just as they'd been in all of Gordon's photos, and Tucker could not look away. Somewhere in the middle of all of this, she'd let go and begun to enjoy the show. Let go and felt the joy in the moment. Had she let go of everything? Had she let go of Gordon?

"Look out," Morgan said, yanking him out of the way of a runaway donkey.

"Distracted just a bit?" Morgan asked, his lip hitching upward.

No sense denying it any longer. "Yeah, I am," Tucker snapped, not at all happy.

Rowdy looked around Morgan at him. "Thought you weren't going to go there."

"Do I look like I planned on it?"

"More like you're having a root canal," Rowdy shot back, eyes serious.

"What are you going to do?" Morgan asked. Both knew the seriousness of what he was facing.

Considering Morgan's question, Tucker watched Abe among the chaos of riders. The kid was doing good, still clinging to the donkey's neck—but one hard buck and he went flying facedown in the dirt. As the donkey ran off, Abe rolled over onto his back.

It took a moment to realize he wasn't getting up.

Tucker bolted toward him the instant he realized it. Running across the arena, he slid to a stop in the dirt, and sank to his knees beside Abe, whose eyes were closed. Suzie came, nearly falling down beside them in her haste to reach her son's side.

"Abe, Abe, speak to me." She grabbed Abe's hand and shook it. When he didn't react she glared at Tucker.

Abe's eyes popped open and a grin spread across his face. "Mom! This has been the best day of my life."

Suzie gasped. "Abe, you scared the dickens out of me."

Tucker stared at the kid, not sure what was going on.

Abe sat up and rubbed his chest. "It's okay, Mom. I just lost my breath for a minute."

"Are you okay now?" Tucker asked, placing a hand on Abe's shoulder. He could feel a crowd gathering behind him.

Abe's grin faded as he studied Tucker and then his mother. "No. I'm not. I've caused a lot of trouble and I'm sorry. I've been thinking about it all night since I talked with the doc yesterday. And—" He paused, straightened his shoulders and met Tucker's gaze. "I need y'all to know that I'm okay. With everything. Tucker, my mom's young. She's going to remarry one day. She said so herself."

Suzie gasped. "Abe Kent, did you hit your head?"

He laughed. "I'm just saying what you told me. And I've been thinking about it. I saw y'all kissing and, well, I was just wondering…if that means y'all love each other. Because if it does, I'm good with it."

"Abe, honey," Suzie said, "I think we need to get you out of the sun."

Tucker pushed his hat back and studied the kid in shock. He agreed wholeheartedly with everything Abe had said, but it was a startling revelation. Standing up, he reached and grabbed the boy beneath the arms. "Here we go, buddy."

"No, I'm fine." Abe scrambled away to stand beside his friends. The boys were all grinning.

"He ain't hit his head," B.J. said. "He's just got his brains back. He done told us he wants Tucker to be his new daddy."

Suzie stood up and stuffed her hands on her hips. "Abe, this is not the way things are supposed to be handled. And you can't just decide you want something and then think that makes it so."

"I know, Mom, but I was thinking that maybe y'all need to know how I feel. So you— So you can both be happy."

"Th-thank you, Abe, but this is not the time or the place to be telling me this."

Suzie looked at Tucker with big, alarmed eyes.

"Okay," he said, having had enough of being the show. "Abe, thanks for speaking your mind. But now everyone needs to get back to what they were doing. Suzie, could you come with me? I think there are a few things we need to talk about." He ignored the excited looks on every boy's face and refrained from looking at his nana. Morgan and Rowdy were grinning like fools.

"We've got it covered," Morgan assured him.

"Yes," Nana said. "Shoo, boys, get on back to your riding."

Tucker glanced at Suzie, but she was already striding out of the arena. He caught up to her just past the trucks. "Suzie, wait. Abe's right, we do need to talk."

She spun around, anger flashing in her eyes. "I've been waiting for you to come talk to me all week. I've been in town, at the shop or at the apartment and you've stayed away. So shoot, I'm ready to hear what you have to say."

He did like the fire in her eyes. "I was giving you time to get settled. I rushed you both times I kissed you, and so I was just biding my time."

She glared at him, but her voice had softened to butter. "Is that so?"

He stepped close but kept his hands to himself. "Yes, it is. Because every time I get near you, I want to hug you up tight and never let you go. I didn't want to chance running you off or worrying Abe again."

She stepped closer to him, lifting her chin so she met his gaze. "So, about this hugging me. Why do you want to do that?"

He cupped her face in his hands. "Because I've fallen completely in love with you, and I'm hoping you'll fall in love with me. And when you're ready to talk about it…I want to—"

To his surprise, Suzie stood on her toes and kissed him. He'd never before been told to stop talking in such a nice way.…

Suzie couldn't help herself and kissed Tucker with all the pent-up love she held for him. He wrapped his arms around her, pulled her close and kissed her deeply. "Tucker," she whispered, drawing away so that she could look at him. "I came to Dew Drop and the Sunrise Ranch as a last resort, because I had no choices. You helped me and Abe come through the fire, and I know he's going to be all right. And much of that was due to you. My life has changed. It was wonderful and it can be wonderful again especially with you in my life."

The most dazzling smile she'd ever seen flashed across Tucker's face. "Then you'll marry me? I love you, Suzie. And I love Abe, and until now I wasn't sure if there was a place for me in y'all's lives."

"I love you so much, Tucker. And Abe is doing great. Whatever happened out in that cave helped free him from the past. He's ready to move forward, and I think he just made it clear that he's ready for you to be a part of our family. And I know without doubt that I am."

"Then, what do you say? Will you make me the happiest man in the world?"

Her heart soared. "Yes."

It was a simple word and it set free the most beautiful promise. Beauty from ashes.

Her life with Gordon had filled her with great joy and happiness, but it wasn't meant to be her future… Life with Tucker was her future.

Wrapping her arms around his neck she kissed him. There were no regrets, no worries, no fears.

Instead there was hope, love and joy.

"I love you, Tucker. I'm so glad you didn't give up on me."

"Never," he assured her, and then kissed her again.

And somewhere in the background she heard clapping—and whoops of glee.

Tucker laughed. "Well, are you ready to go back in there and tell Abe?" Tucker asked, holding her hand gently, his deep blue eyes promising to love her, and cherish her and her son.

"I'm so ready." Holding his hand, she knew she was exactly where she was supposed to be. "I'm so very ready."

As they entered the gate, Abe came jogging their way, a grin plastered across his face and the boys of Sunrise Ranch following him in hot pursuit.

Suzie's heart was so full she had to fight the tears of joy that filled her eyes. "Oh, Tucker, God is so good."

"Yes, darlin', He is."

* * * * *

Dear Reader,

I'm so happy that you chose to visit Sunrise Ranch. I have enjoyed writing this trilogy and telling the stories of the McDermott men and the boys whose lives they've changed at the ranch. Telling Morgan, Rowdy and Tucker's love stories has been a blessing to me. I hope that you've enjoyed them, too, and that the themes have touched you in some way.

I love to hear from readers! To join my newsletter and monthly contest book giveaways, and to keep up with the latest news on me, my website is: www.debraclopton.com

Also, you can drop by my Facebook page at www.facebook.com/debra.clopton.5; check me out on Twitter: @debraclopton; on Goodreads: Debra Clopton; and always by snail mail: Debra Clopton, P.O. Box 1125, Madisonville, TX 77864.

God bless and, until next time, live, laugh and seek God with all your hearts!

Debra Clopton